THE CURSE OF CAMP COLD LAKE

Look for more Goosebumps books
by R.L. Stine:
(see back of book for a complete listing)

Goosebumps®

THE CURSE OF CAMP COLD LAKE

R.L. STINE

AN
APPLE
PAPERBACK

SCHOLASTIC INC.
New York Toronto London Auckland Sydney

A PARACHUTE PRESS BOOK

ISBN 0-590-56893-0

12 11 10 9 8 7 6 5 4 3 2 1   7 8 9/9 0 1 2/0

Printed in the U.S.A.   40

First Scholastic printing, June 1997

THE CURSE OF CAMP COLD LAKE

1

I got off to a bad start at Camp Cold Lake.

I was nervous when I arrived. And I guess I did some dumb things.

Well, I didn't *want* to go to a water sports camp.

I don't like to be outdoors. I *hate* the feeling of grass brushing against my ankles. I don't even like to touch trees. And I certainly don't like getting wet.

Sure, I like to go swimming once in a while. But not *every day*! What's the point of that?

I like to swim in a nice, clean pool. I took one look at the lake here — and I was *sick*. I knew there had to be horrible *things* swimming around in that water.

Ugly creatures, waiting below the surface. Thinking to themselves: "Sarah Maas, we're waiting for you. Sarah, we're going to rub our slimy bodies on your legs when you swim. And we're going to chew off your toes, one by one."

1

Yuck. Why do I have to swim in *slime*?

Of course, Aaron was so excited, he nearly exploded.

When we climbed off the camp bus, he was jumping up and down and talking a mile a minute. He was so crazed. I thought he was going to burst out of his clothes and go running into the lake!

My brother likes camp. He likes sports and the outdoors. He likes just about everything and everyone.

And everyone always likes Aaron. He's so enthusiastic. He's so much *fun*.

Hey — I like to have fun too. But how can you have fun when there are no malls, no movie theaters, no restaurants to get a slice of pizza or a bag of french fries?

How can you have fun up to your neck in a freezing cold lake every day? In a camp miles from any town? Surrounded on all sides by thick woods?

"This is going to be awesome!" Aaron declared. Dragging his duffel bag, he hurried off to find his cabin.

"Yeah. Awesome," I muttered glumly. The bright sun was already making me sweat.

Do I like to sweat? Of course not.

So why did I come to Camp Cold Lake? I can answer that in three words: Mom and Dad.

They said that a water sports camp would give me confidence. They said it would help make me more comfortable with the outdoors.

And they said it would give me a chance to make new friends.

Okay, I admit it. I don't make friends easily. I'm not like Aaron. I can't just walk up to someone and start talking and kidding around.

I'm a little shy. Maybe it's because I'm so much taller than everyone else. I'm a whole head taller than Aaron. And he's only a year younger than I am. He's eleven.

I'm tall and very skinny. Sometimes Dad calls me "Grasshopper."

Guess how much I like that.

About as much as I like swimming in a cold lake filled with hidden creatures.

"Be a good sport about it, Sarah," Mom said.

I rolled my eyes.

"Give camp a chance," Dad added. "You might surprise yourself and have a good time."

I rolled my eyes again.

"When you come home at the end of summer, you'll probably beg us to take you camping!" Dad joked.

I wanted to roll my eyes again — but they were getting tired from all that rolling.

I gave my parents a glum sigh. Quick hugs. Then I followed Aaron onto the camp bus.

He grinned the whole way to camp. He was really excited about learning how to water-ski. And he kept asking everyone if the camp had a high diving board over the lake.

Aaron made three or four good friends on the bus ride to camp.

I stared out the window, watching the endless blur of trees and farms. Thinking about my lucky friends who got to stay home and hang out at the mall.

Then here we were at Camp Cold Lake. Kids pulling their bags off the bus. Laughing and joking. Counselors in dark green T-shirts greeting everyone, pointing them in the right direction.

I began to cheer up a little bit.

Maybe I *will* make some new friends, I thought. Maybe I'll meet some kids who are a lot like me — and we'll have a great summer.

But then I stepped into my cabin. I saw my three bunk mates. I looked around.

And I let out a cry. "Oh, no! No way!"

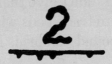

2

I guess I shouldn't have freaked like that.

It made a very bad first impression.

But what was I supposed to do?

There were two bunk beds in the cabin. The three other girls had already chosen their beds. There was only one bed left — right in front of the window.

And the window had no screens.

Which meant that my bed would be *crawling* with bugs. I took one glance — and I knew I'd be swatting mosquitoes every night for the whole summer.

Besides, I can't sleep in a top bunk. I toss and turn a lot at night. If I slept on top, I'd fall on my head.

I had to sleep on the bottom. In the bed against the far wall, away from the open window.

"I — I can't do this!" I blurted out.

My three bunk mates turned to look at me. One had blond hair pulled back in a ponytail. Near her

5

was a short, chubby girl with long brown hair. In the bottom bunk against the wall, an African-American girl with long cornrows stared across the cabin at me.

I guess they wanted to say hi and introduce themselves. But I didn't give them a chance.

"Someone has to trade beds with me!" I cried. I didn't mean to sound so shrill. But I was really upset.

Before they could answer, the cabin door swung open. A sandy-haired young guy in a dark green camp T-shirt poked his head in.

"I'm Richard," he said. "I'm the boss guy, the head dude. Everything okay in here?"

"No!" I cried.

I couldn't stop myself. I was just so nervous and unhappy. "I can't sleep in this bunk!" I told him. "I don't want to be near the window. And I need to sleep on the bottom."

I could see that the other girls were shocked by my outburst.

Richard turned to the girl who was sitting on the bottom bunk against the wall. "Briana, would you trade beds with —"

"Sarah," I told him.

"Would you trade bunks with Sarah?" Richard asked Briana.

She shook her head so hard, the beads in her cornrows rattled against each other. "I really don't want to," she said softly.

6

She pointed to the chubby girl with long brown hair, who sat on a camp trunk. "Meg and I were bunk mates last year," Briana told Richard. "And we kind of wanted to be together."

Meg nodded. She had a round, baby face. Squirrel cheeks out to here. And she wore blue and red braces on her teeth.

"I can't sleep in front of the window," I insisted. "I really can't. I hate bugs."

Richard stared hard at Briana. "How about it?"

Briana groaned. "Oh . . . all right." She made a face at me.

"Thanks," Richard said. I could see he was studying me.

He probably thinks I'm a real troublemaker, I thought.

Briana climbed off the bottom bunk. She dragged her duffel bag across the room to the bunk by the window. "It's all yours," she muttered.

She didn't say it in a friendly way.

I felt bad. My bunk mates hate me already, I thought.

Why do I always do that? Why do I always get nervous and start off on the wrong foot with people?

Now I've got to try really hard to make them my friends, I decided.

But a minute later, I did something horrible.

3

"Hey — thanks for trading bunks, Briana," I said. "That was really nice of you."

She nodded but didn't say anything. Meg pulled open her trunk and started shoving shorts and T-shirts into her dresser drawer.

The third girl smiled at me. "Hi. I'm Janice," she said. She had a raspy, hoarse voice. "Everyone calls me Jan."

Jan had a nice smile. She had her blond hair pulled back in a ponytail. She had dark blue eyes and red cheeks. She seemed to be blushing all the time.

"Were you here last summer?" I asked her.

She shook her head. "No. Briana and Meg were here. But this is my first summer. I went to tennis camp last year."

"I've never been to any kind of camp," I confessed. "I — I guess I'm a little nervous."

"Are you a good swimmer?" Briana asked.

I shrugged. "Pretty good, I guess. I don't swim much. I don't really like it."

Meg turned from her trunk. "You don't like to swim, and you came to a water sports camp?"

Briana and Jan laughed.

I could feel my face grow hot. I didn't want to tell them that my parents *made* me come to this camp. That just sounded too geeky. I didn't know *what* to say.

"I . . . uh . . . I like other things," I stammered.

"Oh — I *love* that swimsuit!" Briana declared. She pulled a bright yellow swimsuit from Meg's trunk and held it up in front of her. "This is excellent!"

Meg tugged it back. "Like it would really fit you!" she muttered, rolling her eyes. Her braces clicked when she talked.

Meg looked a little like a bowling ball next to tall, graceful Briana.

"Did you lose weight over the winter?" Briana asked her. "You look great. Really, Meg."

"I lost a little," Meg replied. She sighed. "But I didn't get any taller."

"I grew about a foot this year," I chimed in. "I'm the tallest girl in my school. Everyone stares at me when I walk through the halls."

"Boo hoo," Meg said sarcastically. "You've really got it tough. Would you rather be a shrimp like me?"

"Well . . . not really," I replied.

Ooops. I realized I'd said the wrong thing.

I saw a flash of hurt in Meg's eyes.

Why did I say that? I asked myself.

Why do I keep putting my foot in my mouth?

I picked up my backpack from where I had tossed it on the floor. I carried it to my bunk to unpack it.

"Hey — that's mine! Put it down!" Jan came rushing over to me.

I glanced down at the backpack. "No. It's mine," I insisted.

I started to unzip it — and it fell off the bed.

A whole bunch of things fell out and clattered across the cabin floor.

"Oh!" I cried out in surprise. The stuff *wasn't* mine.

I saw pill bottles. Medicine jars. And little plastic inhalers.

"Asthma medicine?" I cried.

Jan dropped to her knees and began gathering it all up. She glared up at me angrily. "Thanks a bunch, Sarah," she growled. "Thanks for letting the whole world know I have asthma. Why don't you stand up at the campfire tonight and announce it to the whole camp?"

"Sorry," I murmured weakly.

"I *told* you it was *my* backpack," Jan snapped.

Meg bent down and picked up an inhaler for Jan.

"Having asthma is nothing to be ashamed of," she told Jan.

"Maybe I like to keep some things to myself," Jan snapped. She shoved all the medicine into the pocket and grabbed the backpack away.

"Sorry," I said again. "Really."

All three girls glared at me. Briana shook her head. Meg *tsk-tsk*ed.

They hate me already, I thought.

I felt sick. Really sick.

They hate me, and it's only the first day. The first *hour*.

With a sigh, I slumped down on my bunk.

Can things get any worse? I wondered.

Guess the answer to that.

4

Later that night, we had our first campfire. It was built in a wide, flat clearing near the woods. Smooth logs were placed in a circle to be used as benches.

I dropped down on an empty log with my back to the trees. Flames from the big fire danced brightly against the gray evening sky.

The fire crackled and popped. It smelled so sweet. I took a deep breath.

Counselors tossed more sticks on the fire. Soon the flames rose up over their heads.

The night air was hot and dry. My cheeks burned from the heat tossed off by the fire.

I turned away and gazed into the woods. The dark trees shivered in a light breeze. In the gray light, I saw a squirrel dart between tall weeds.

I wondered what other animals lurked in the woods. I imagined there were bigger animals than squirrels in there. Bigger and more dangerous.

A loud *POP* from the fire made me jump.

It's creepy outside at night, I thought. Why can't they have the campfire indoors? In a fireplace or something.

I slapped a mosquito on my neck.

When I turned back to the fire, I saw Briana and Meg on another log bench. They were laughing about something. Talking to two girls I didn't know.

I saw Aaron on the other side of the flames. He was goofing with two other guys. They were wrestling around, trying to shove each other off the log.

I sighed. Aaron has already made a bunch of friends, I thought.

Everyone has made friends — but me.

Aaron saw me staring at him. He waved quickly, then turned back to his friends.

On the next log, three girls had their heads tossed back. They were loudly singing the camp song.

I listened carefully, trying to learn the words. But they had a giggling fit halfway through and didn't finish the song.

Two older girls sat down on the other end of my log. They looked about fifteen or sixteen. I turned to say hi to them. But they were busy talking.

One of them had a bag of Gummi Worms in her hand. She kept pulling them out of the bag one by one and slurping them slowly like spaghetti noodles.

Richard, the head counselor, stepped in front of the fire. He had a black baseball cap turned backwards on his head. His baggy shorts were torn and dirty from working on the fire.

He raised both hands over his head. "Are we all here?" he called out.

I could barely hear him. Everyone was still talking and laughing. Across the fire, I saw Aaron standing up, wiggling his whole body in a funny dance.

His friends were laughing their heads off. One of them slapped Aaron a high five.

"Can we get started?" Richard called out. "Can we start our welcoming campfire?"

A log cracked in the fire. Red embers shot up all around.

"Oh!" I let out a cry as a hand grabbed my shoulder.

"Who — ?" I spun around, startled. And stared up at Briana and Meg.

They leaned over me. In the darting firelight, I saw their frightened expressions.

"Sarah — run!" Briana whispered.

"Get up — quick!" Meg tugged my arm. "Run!"

"Why? What's wrong?" I sputtered.

5

I jumped shakily to my feet. "What's wrong?"

"Those boys," Meg whispered. She pointed across the fire. "They threw fireworks in the fire! It's going to explode!"

"Run!" both girls cried.

Meg gave me a shove to get me started.

I stumbled — and then lurched forward. As I ran, I shut my eyes tight, expecting the blast any second.

Could I get away in time? Were Meg and Briana escaping it too?

I stopped short when I heard the laughter.

Shrill, gleeful laughter.

"Huh?" Swallowing hard, I turned back.

And saw half the camp laughing at me.

Meg and Briana slapped each other a high five.

"No. Oh, noooo," I murmured. How could I fall for such a dumb trick?

How could they play such a mean joke on me?

15

They must have told everyone to watch. As I stood at the edge of the clearing by myself, I could feel all the eyes on me.

And I could hear kids laughing and making jokes.

I saw Jan laughing. And I saw Richard and some of the other counselors grinning and shaking their heads.

I know, I know. I should have laughed too. I should have made a joke of it.

I shouldn't have let it upset me.

But the whole day had been so terrible. I was so nervous. And so eager not to make any more mistakes.

I could feel my shoulders start to shake up and down. I could feel tears welling up in my eyes.

No! I ordered myself. You *cannot* cry! You cannot allow yourself to cry in front of the whole camp.

Sure, you feel like a total jerk, Sarah. But so what? It was just a joke. Just a dumb joke.

I felt a hand on my arm. I pulled away.

"Sarah —" Aaron stood beside me. His dark eyes were wide in the shadowy evening light.

"I'm okay," I snapped. "Go away."

"You're such a bad sport," he said softly. "Why can't you ever let things slide off you? It was just a joke. Why go nuts over a dumb joke?"

Do you know what I really hate?

I really hate it when Aaron is right.

16

I mean, he's my younger brother — right? What right does he have to be the sensible, calm member of the Maas family?

It really steams me when Aaron comes on like the *older* brother.

"Do I need your advice?" I snarled. "Take a hike." I gave him a shove toward the campfire.

He shrugged and hurried back to his friends.

I crept to the campfire. I didn't go to my old seat. It was too close to the fire — and too close to Briana and Meg.

I dropped down on the edge of a log near the woods, outside the glow of the fire. The darkness cooled me and helped to calm me down.

Richard had been talking for a while. I realized I hadn't heard a word he said.

He stood in front of the crackling fire. He had a deep, booming voice. But everyone leaned in to hear him better.

I gazed around the circle of campers. Their faces glowed orange in the bright firelight. Their eyes sparkled.

I wondered if anyone here would be my friend.

I knew I was feeling really sorry for myself. I wondered if any other new campers felt the way I did.

Richard's voice droned on in the back of my mind. He was saying something about the main lodge. Something about the meal schedule. Then he began talking about towels.

I started to pay attention when he introduced the head waterfront counselor. Her name was Liz.

Everyone clapped when she stood up beside Richard. One of the boys gave a loud wolf whistle.

"She's awesome!" another boy called out.

Everyone laughed.

Liz grinned too. She knew she looked really awesome. She wore tight denim cutoffs and a dark blue midriff top. She waved for everyone to get quiet.

"Are you all having a good time?" she called out.

Everyone cheered and clapped. Several boys whistled.

"Well, tomorrow will be your first day at the waterfront," Liz announced. "And before you go in the lake, there are lots of water rules we want you to know."

"Like, don't drink the water!" Richard chimed in. "Unless you're *very* thirsty!"

Some kids laughed. I didn't. The thought of drinking that disgusting, slimy water made me sick.

Liz didn't laugh, either. She frowned at Richard. "We need to take this seriously," she scolded.

"I *was* serious!" Richard joked.

Liz ignored him. "When you get back to your bunks, you will find a list of water rules on your bed," she continued, brushing back her long, frizzy red hair. "There are twenty rules on the list. And you need to know them all."

Huh? *Twenty* rules? I thought. How can there be twenty rules?

It will take all summer to learn twenty rules.

Liz held up a sheet of paper. "I'm going to go over the list with you now. If you have any questions, just call them out."

"Can we go swimming now?" a boy shouted, trying to be funny.

Lots of kids laughed.

But Liz didn't crack a smile. "That's rule number eight," she replied. "No night swimming, even if counselors are with you."

"Don't *ever* swim with counselors!" Richard joked. "They have germs!"

Richard is pretty funny, I thought. He seems like a good guy.

But Liz seems so *serious*.

The sheet of paper fluttered in the wind. She gripped it with both hands. Her red hair caught the glow of the fire.

"The most important rule at Camp Cold Lake is the Buddy System," Liz announced. "When you are in the lake, you must always have a buddy."

She glanced quickly at the campers seated around her. "Even if you are only wading in up to your ankles, you must have a swimming buddy with you," she said. "You may have a different buddy each time. Or you may choose a buddy for the whole summer. But you must *always* have a buddy."

She took a deep breath. "Are there any questions?"

"Will *you* be my buddy?" a boy shouted.

Everyone laughed. I laughed too. The kid's timing was perfect.

But once again, Liz didn't crack a smile. "As waterfront counselor, I will act as *everyone's* buddy," she replied seriously.

"Now, rule number two," she continued. "Never swim more than three boat lengths from one of our safety boats. Rule number three — no shouting or pretending to be in trouble in the water. No horseplay. No kidding around. Rule number four . . ."

She talked on and on, reading off all twenty rules.

I groaned. She talks to us like we're five year olds, I thought.

And there are so many water rules.

"Let me repeat one more time about the Buddy System . . . ," Liz was saying.

Gazing past the fire, I could see the dark lake. Smooth and black and silent.

The lake has tiny waves. No current. No dangerous tides.

So *why* are there so many rules? I wondered. What are they scared of?

6

Liz talked for at least half an hour. Richard kept cracking jokes, trying to make her laugh. But she never even smiled.

She talked some more about every rule on the list. Then she told us to read the list carefully when we got back to our cabins.

"Have a safe summer, everyone!" she called out. "See you at the waterfront!"

Everyone cheered and whistled again as Liz stepped away from the fire. I yawned and stretched my hands over my head. That was really boring, I thought.

I've never heard of a place having so many rules.

I swatted another mosquito on my neck. I was starting to feel really itchy. That's what being outdoors does to me. It makes me itch like crazy.

The fire had died down. A blanket of purple embers glowed on the dark ground. The night air grew cool.

To end the campfire, Richard told everyone to stand and sing the camp song. "You new campers probably don't know the words," he said. "You're *lucky*!"

Everyone laughed. Then Richard began to sing, and everyone joined in.

I tried to follow along. But I couldn't catch all of the words. I picked up pieces of the song. . . .

"Wetter is better . . ."

"Get in the swim.
Show your vigor and vim . . ."

"Every son and daughter
should be in the water,
the cold, cold water
of Camp Cold Lake."

Yuck. I agreed with Richard about the words to the song. They were so lame!

Gazing across the fire, I saw Aaron singing his heart out. He seemed to know every word already.

How does he do it? I wondered, scratching my itchy legs. How does he manage to be so perfect? To fit in everywhere?

As the song ended, Richard raised his hands for quiet. "I have a few final announcements," he called out. "First of all, none of you can carry a tune! Second . . ."

I didn't hear the rest. I turned to find Briana and Meg standing beside me.

I took a step back. "What do you want?" I snapped.

"We want to apologize," Briana said.

Meg nodded. "Yeah. We're sorry we played that dumb joke on you."

Richard's voice droned on behind us. Briana put a hand on my shoulder. "We got off to a bad start," she said. "Let's start all over again. Okay, Sarah?"

"Yeah. Let's start fresh," Meg agreed.

A smile spread over my face. "Great," I said. "Excellent."

"Excellent!" Briana repeated, smiling too.

She slapped me on the back. "A fresh start!"

Richard was still making announcements. "Tomorrow at four-thirty, those interested in windsurfing . . ."

Aaron will probably try that, I thought. I watched Briana and Meg walk away.

A fresh start, I thought. I began to feel a lot happier.

The happy feeling lasted for about two seconds.

Then my back started to itch.

I turned to the fire and saw Briana and Meg staring back at me. They were both giggling.

Other kids had turned away from Richard and were watching me.

"Ohhhh." I groaned when I felt something warm wriggle against my back.

Something warm and dry, moving under my T-shirt.

"Ohhhh." It moved again.

I reached one hand back. And poked it under my shirt.

What is it? What did Briana put back there?

I grabbed the thing and pulled it out.

And started to scream.

7

The snake wriggled in my hand.

It looked like a long black shoelace. With eyes! And a mouth that kept snapping open and shut.

"Noooooo!" I totally lost it.

I let out a shrill scream. And I heaved the snake with all my might.

It sailed into the woods.

My back still itched like crazy. I could still feel it wriggling against my skin.

I reached back and tried to scratch with both hands.

Kids were laughing. Telling each other what Briana had done.

I didn't care. I just wanted to rub away the feeling of that snake against my skin.

My whole body tingled. I uttered an angry cry. "How *could* you?" I shrieked at Briana and Meg. "What is your *problem*?"

Aaron came hurrying over to be the grown-up again.

Just what I needed. Mr. Mature Kid Brother.

"Sarah, did it bite you?" he asked softly.

I shook my head. "I can still feel it!" I wailed. "Did you see it? It was three feet long!"

"Calm down," Aaron whispered. "Everyone is staring at you."

"Think I don't know it?" I snapped.

"Well, it was just a tiny snake," Aaron said. "Totally harmless. Try to get yourself together."

"I — I — I —" I sputtered. I was too upset, too angry to talk.

Aaron raised his eyes to Briana and Meg. "Why are those two girls picking on you?" he asked.

"I don't know!" I wailed. "Because . . . because they're *creeps*! That's why!"

"Well, try to calm down," Aaron repeated. "Look at you, Sarah. You're shaking all over."

"You'd shake too if you had a disgusting snake crawling up and down your skin!" I replied. "And I really don't need your advice, Aaron. I really don't —"

"Fine," he replied. He spun away and hurried back to his friends.

"I don't believe him," I muttered.

Dad is a doctor, and Aaron is just like him. He thinks he has to take care of everyone in the world.

Well, I can take care of myself. I don't need my little brother telling me to calm down every second.

26

Richard was still talking. But I didn't care. I stepped away from the campfire circle and started back to the cabin.

The path curved through a patch of woods, up the sloping hill where the cabins were perched. Away from the glow of the fire, I was surrounded by darkness.

I clicked on my flashlight and aimed the yellow circle of light at my feet. My sneakers crunched over dry leaves and twigs. The trees whispered above me.

How did I get off to such a bad start? I asked myself.

Why do Briana and Meg hate me so much?

Maybe they're just mean, I decided. Maybe they're total creeps. Maybe they're mean to everyone.

They think they're so hot because they were at camp last year.

Without realizing it, I had wandered off the path. "Hey —" I swung the flashlight around, searching for the way back.

The light swept over tilting trees, tall clumps of weeds, a fallen log.

Panic tightened my throat.

Where is the path? Where?

I took a few steps. My sneaker crunched over leaves.

And then my foot sank into something soft.

Quicksand!

27

8

No. Not quicksand.

There's no such thing as quicksand. I remembered that from some science book I read in fifth grade.

I lowered the flashlight.

"Ohhhh." Mud. Thick, gooey mud.

My sneaker sank deep into the ooze.

I pulled my leg up with a groan — and nearly toppled over backwards.

It's just mud, I told myself. It's disgusting — but it's no big deal.

But then I saw the spiders.

Dozens of them. The biggest spiders I ever saw.

There must have been a nest of them in the mud.

They were crawling over my shoe, crawling up the leg of my jeans.

"Ohhhh. Yuck!"

Dozens of spiders clung to me. I shook my

sneaker. Hard. Then I began batting at them with my free hand.

"*I hate this caaaaaamp!*" I screamed.

I beat some spiders away with the flashlight.

And then I had an idea.

I mean, why shouldn't I pay Briana and Meg back for what they did to me?

They embarrassed me in front of the whole camp. And I hardly did anything to them.

I emptied the batteries from the flashlight. I took a deep breath. Then I bent down — and scooped a bunch of spiders into the flashlight.

Yuck. I felt sick. I really did.

I mean, can you imagine — *me* handling spiders!

But I knew it would be worth it. Soon.

I filled the flashlight with the squirming, black creatures. Then I screwed on the top.

I stepped over a fallen tree trunk. Found the path. And carrying the flashlight carefully, I eagerly hurried to the cabin.

I stopped outside the door. The lights were on inside the cabin.

I peeked in through the open window. No. No sign of anyone.

I crept inside.

I pulled up the blanket on Briana's bed. Then I emptied half of the spiders onto her sheet. I carefully pulled the blanket over them and smoothed it out.

I was pouring the rest of the spiders into Meg's bed when I heard a shuffling noise behind me. Quickly, I pulled Meg's blanket back into place and spun around.

Jan stepped into the cabin. "What's up?" she asked in her hoarse, croaky voice.

"Nothing," I replied, hiding the flashlight behind my back.

Jan yawned. "It's Lights Out in ten minutes," she said.

I glanced at Briana's bunk. I'd left one corner of the blanket untucked. Briana won't notice, I decided.

I realized I was grinning. I quickly changed my expression. I didn't want Jan asking a lot of questions.

She turned and pulled a long white nightshirt from her dresser drawer. "What did you sign up for tomorrow?" she asked. "Free Swim?"

"No. Canoeing," I told her.

I wanted to be in a nice, dry canoe. Not flopping around in the dirty lake with fish and other slimy creatures.

"Hey. Me too," Jan said.

I started to ask if she would be my buddy. But Briana and Meg came strolling through the door.

They saw me — and burst out laughing.

"What was that wild dance you were doing at the campfire?" Briana teased.

"You looked as if you had a snake down your back or something!" Meg declared.

They laughed some more.

That's okay, I thought. Go ahead and laugh.

In a few minutes, when you climb under your covers, *I'll* be laughing.

I couldn't wait.

9

A few minutes later, Jan turned out the lights. I lay on the hard mattress, staring up at Meg's mattress above my head, grinning. Waiting . . .

Waiting . . .

Meg shifted her weight in the bunk above me.

I heard her gasp.

And then both Briana and Meg began to scream.

I laughed out loud. I couldn't hold it in.

"It bit me! It *bit* me!" Briana howled.

The lights flashed on.

"Help!" Meg cried. She leaped out of bed. Her bare feet hit the floor hard. It sounded like an elephant landing.

"It bit me!" Briana cried.

She and Meg were both on the floor now, dancing and wriggling. Slapping at their arms, their legs, their backs.

I bit my lip to make myself stop laughing.

"Spiders! Spiders all over!" Meg shrieked. "Ow!

It bit me too!" She pulled up the sleeve of her nightshirt. "Ow! That hurts!"

Jan stood at the light switch. I hadn't moved from my bed. I was enjoying it all too much. Watching them squirm and dance.

But Jan's words wiped the smile from my face.

"Sarah put the spiders there," she told Briana and Meg. "I saw her messing around at your bunks when I came in."

What a snitch. I guess she was still angry at me because I spilled her asthma medicine.

Well, that put an end to the fun.

I think Briana and Meg wanted to strangle me. They both had to go to the infirmary and wake up the camp nurse. They had to make sure the spider bites weren't poisonous.

How was I to know that these were the kind of spiders that bite?

It was just a joke, after all.

I tried to apologize when they came trudging back from the nurse. But they wouldn't speak to me. And neither would Jan.

Oh, well, I sighed. So they won't be my friends. I'll make other friends. . . .

The next morning in the mess hall, I ate breakfast alone. The room had two long tables that stretched from wall to wall. One for boys and one for girls.

33

I sat at the far end of the girls' table and spooned up my cornflakes in silence.

All the other girls were chattering away. At the other end of the table, Briana and Meg kept flashing me angry looks.

I saw Aaron at the boys' table. He and his friends were laughing and goofing on each other. Aaron balanced a pancake on his forehead. Another boy slapped it off.

At least *he's* having fun, I thought bitterly.

I had the sudden urge to go over and tell Aaron how unhappy I was. But I knew he would just tell me to lighten up.

So I sat at my lonely end of the table and choked down my cornflakes.

Did things get better when I arrived at the lake for canoeing?

Three guesses.

Kids were already pulling their canoes off the grassy shore, into the water. They all seemed to be paired up.

Liz walked over to me. Her white one-piece bathing suit glowed in the morning sunlight. She had her frizzy red hair tied behind her head.

She let a silver whistle fall from her mouth. "What's your name?" she asked, eyes on the lake.

"Sarah," I told her. "I signed up for canoeing, but —"

"You need a buddy," she said. "Find a buddy.

34

The canoes are over there." She pointed, then trotted away.

Canoes splashed into the water. The slap of the wooden paddles echoed around the shore.

I ran to the stack of canoes, searching for a buddy. But everyone had already chosen partners.

I was about to give up when I spotted Jan, pulling a canoe to the water. "Do you have a buddy?" I called.

She shook her head.

"Well, can I come with you?" I asked.

"I don't think so," she replied nastily. "Do you have any more spiders you want to set loose?"

"Jan, please —" I started.

"Are you two together?" Liz appeared behind us, startling us both.

"No. I —" Jan started.

"I *want* to be her buddy, but she doesn't want to," I said. I didn't mean to whine, but it came out that way.

Jan made an ugly face at me.

"Get your canoe in the water," Liz ordered. "You two are the last ones in."

Jan started to protest. Then she shrugged and sighed. "Okay, Sarah. Let's go."

We pulled on life preservers. Then I grabbed a paddle and one end of the canoe. We dragged it to the water.

The little boat bobbed against the shore. The

lake current was stronger than I thought. Low waves plopped steadily against the grassy shore.

Jan climbed in and took a seat in the front. "Thanks for embarrassing me in front of Liz," she muttered.

"I didn't mean —" I started.

"Okay. Push off," she commanded.

I tossed my paddle into the canoe. Then I leaned over and gave the boat a hard shove with both hands.

It slid smoothly away from the shore. Then I had to wade out to it and pull myself inside.

"Whoa!" As I struggled to hoist myself up, the canoe nearly tipped over.

"Watch it!" Jan snapped. "You're such a klutz, Sarah."

"Sorry," I murmured. I was so grateful to have a buddy, I didn't want any more trouble between us.

I pulled myself into the canoe and dropped down behind Jan.

The canoe bobbed up and down as we began to paddle. The rocking waters sparkled like silver under the bright morning sunshine.

It took us a while to find the right rhythm.

Neither of us spoke.

The slap of our paddles and the rush of water against the little canoe were the only sounds we made.

The lake gleamed in front of us like a giant,

round mirror. I could see several canoes up ahead. Jan and I were far behind them.

The rubber life preservers were hot and heavy. We pulled them off and dropped them to the canoe floor.

We paddled steadily, not too fast, not too slow.

I glanced back. The shore seemed miles away.

I felt a chill of fear. I'm not that strong a swimmer. I suddenly wondered if I could swim all the way to shore from out here.

"Hey!" As I stared back at the shore, the canoe suddenly started to rock.

"Whoooa!" I grabbed the sides.

I turned — and to my horror, saw Jan *standing up*!

"Jan — stop! What are you doing?" I shrieked. *"What are you doing?"*

The little boat rocked harder. I gripped the sides, struggling to steady it.

Jan took a step.

The canoe tilted. Water splashed over my feet.

"Jan — stop!" I cried again. "Sit down! What are you *doing*?"

She narrowed her eyes at me. "Bye, Sarah."

10

The boat tilted more as she raised one foot to the side. She pulled off the T-shirt she had over her swimsuit and tossed it to the canoe floor.

"No — please!" I begged. "Don't leave me out here. I'm not a good swimmer. What if the boat tips over? I don't think I can swim back from here!"

"You ruined my summer," she accused. "Now everyone knows I have asthma. So they won't let me go on the six-day canoe trip."

"But — but it was an accident —" I sputtered.

"And you're messing up everything for Briana and Meg too," Jan said angrily.

"No. Wait —" I started. "I apologized to them. I didn't mean —"

She shifted her weight.

Tilted the canoe the other way.

Then she shifted her weight again. Again.

Deliberately making the canoe rock.

Deliberately trying to frighten me.

"Don't tip it over, Jan. Please —" I pleaded.

She tilted it more. Made it rock so hard, I thought I'd tumble out.

"I'm really not a good swimmer," I repeated. "I really don't think I —"

She uttered a disgusted groan. Then she tossed back her hair. Raised her arms over her head. Bent her knees. Kicked off hard.

And dove into the lake.

"Noooo!" I let out a cry as the boat rocked violently. Jan's dive sent up a tall, foamy wave of water.

The canoe tilted . . . rocked . . .

. . . and flipped over!

I hit with a *smack*. Cold water rose up around me as I sank.

Frozen in shock.

I felt the canoe bounce above me on the surface.

Then I started to choke as water invaded my nose and mouth.

Sputtering and gagging, I thrashed my arms and legs.

Pushed myself . . . pushed . . . pushed myself to the surface.

And raised my head over the bobbing current.

Still sputtering, I sucked in a deep breath of fresh air. Then another.

Floating on the surface, I saw the canoe bobbing upside down on the water.

I struggled to catch my breath, to slow my racing heart.

Then I swam to the canoe. I grabbed on to it. Wrapped one arm around it. Held on for dear life.

Bobbing with the canoe, I squinted into the sunlight, searching for Jan.

"Jan? Jan?" I called to her.

"Jan? Where *are* you?"

I turned and searched in all directions.

A feeling of cold dread tightened my chest.

"Jan? Jan? Can you hear me?" I shouted.

11

I held on to the canoe with one hand and shielded my eyes with the other. "Jan? Jan?" I shouted her name as loudly as I could.

And then I spotted her.

I saw her blond hair glowing in the bright sunlight. And I saw her red swimsuit. Her arms moving steadily, smoothly. Her feet kicking up foamy waves.

She was making her way to shore.

She swam away and left me here, I realized.

I turned and searched for the other canoes. Squinting against the sun, I could see them far ahead of me. Too far away to hear my shouts.

Maybe I can turn the canoe over, I decided. Then I can climb in and paddle back to shore.

But where were the paddles?

I raised my eyes to the camp — and saw Jan talking to Liz. She was waving her arms frantically and pointing out to the water. Pointing to me.

A crowd of kids gathered around them. I could hear excited voices. Shouts and cries.

I saw Liz pull a canoe into the water.

She's coming to rescue me, I realized. Jan must have told her I couldn't swim all the way back.

I suddenly felt embarrassed. I knew all the kids onshore were watching me. I knew they were talking about what a wimp I must be.

But I didn't care. I just wanted to get back on dry land.

It didn't take Liz long to paddle out to me. When I pulled myself into the canoe, I started to thank her.

But she didn't let me get a word out. "Why did you do it, Sarah?" she demanded.

"Excuse me?" I gasped. "Do what?"

"Why did you tip the canoe over?" Liz asked.

I opened my mouth to protest — but only a squeak came out.

Liz frowned at me. "Jan says you deliberately tipped over the canoe. Don't you know how dangerous that is, Sarah?"

"But — but — but —!"

"I'm calling a special camp meeting because of this," Liz said. "Water safety is so important. The water safety rules must be followed at all times. Camp Cold Lake couldn't exist if campers didn't follow every rule."

"I wish it *didn't* exist," I muttered unhappily.

So Liz held a long meeting at the lodge. And everyone at camp had to be there.

She went over the rules of water safety again. Rule by rule.

And then she showed an endless slide show about the Buddy System.

I sat way on the side and stared down at the floor. But every time I raised my eyes, I saw Briana, Meg, and Jan glaring angrily at me.

Other campers kept staring at me too. I guess they all blamed me for this long, boring meeting. Jan probably told everyone in camp that I was the one who tipped over the canoe.

"I want you to memorize all twenty water safety rules," Liz was saying.

More campers stared angrily at me.

Everyone hates me, I thought, shaking my head sadly. And there is nothing I can do about it.

Then, suddenly, I had an idea.

12

"I'm going to run away," I told Aaron.

"Good-bye," he said calmly. "Good luck."

"No. Really!" I insisted. "I'm not kidding. I'm really going to run away from this camp."

"Send me a postcard," Aaron said.

I had dragged him away from the mess hall after dinner. I really needed to talk to him. I pulled him to the edge of the lake.

No one else was down here. Everyone was still at the mess hall in the lodge.

I glanced at the canoes, stacked in piles of three near the water. I pictured Jan's blond hair, her red swimsuit. I pictured her swimming away, leaving me in the middle of the lake.

And then lying to Liz. Getting me in trouble. . . .

I shook Aaron by the shoulders. "Why won't you take me seriously?" I cried through clenched teeth.

He laughed.

"You shouldn't shake a person after they've

just eaten the camp meat loaf." He let out a loud burp.

"You're so gross." I groaned.

He grinned. "It's a family tradition."

"Stop joking around. I mean it," I snapped. "I'm really unhappy, Aaron. I hate this camp. There is no phone here we can use. I can't call Mom and Dad. So I'm going to run away."

His expression changed. He saw that I was serious.

He skipped a flat stone across the water. I watched the ripples spread out, then disappear.

The lake reflected the gray evening sky. Everything was gray. The ground, the sky, the water. Reflections of trees shimmered darkly in the gray water.

"Where are you going to run?" Aaron asked softly. I could see him quickly becoming the mature, "wiser" brother again. But I didn't care.

I had to tell him my plan. I couldn't leave camp without letting him know.

"Through the woods," I said. I pointed. "There is a town on the other side of the woods. When I get to the town, I'm going to call Mom and Dad and tell them to come get me."

"You can't!" Aaron protested.

I stuck my chin out. "Why not?"

"We're not allowed in the woods," he replied. "Richard said the woods were dangerous — remember?"

45

I shoved Aaron again. I was so tense, so angry, I didn't know what to do with my hands.

"I don't care what Richard said!" I bellowed. "I'm running away — remember?"

"Give the camp a chance, Sarah," Aaron urged. "We haven't even been here a whole week. Give the place a chance."

That's when I totally lost it.

"I *hate* it when you're so sensible!" I screamed.

I shoved him hard. With both hands.

His mouth flew open. He lost his balance — and toppled into the lake.

He landed on his back in the wet mud just past the shore.

"Ooof!" I heard the air shoot out of him.

"Sorry —" I started. "It was an accident, Aaron. I —"

He scrambled to his feet, pulling up greasy gunk and seaweed with him. Shaking his fists. Calling me all kinds of names.

I sighed. Now even my brother was furious at me.

What am I going to do? I asked myself. What *can* I do?

As I trudged back to the cabin, another plan began to form in my mind.

A really desperate plan.

A really *dangerous* plan.

"Tomorrow," I murmured to myself, "I'm going to show them all!"

46

13

I thought about my plan all the next morning. I was frightened — but I knew I had to go through with it.

Our group had Free Swim that afternoon. Of course, everyone had a buddy but me.

I dug my bare feet into the muddy shore and watched everyone pair up and head into the water. Puffy white clouds floated overhead, reflected in the nearly still water.

Tiny gnats jumped over the surface of the water. I stared at them, wondering why they didn't get wet.

"Sarah, it's swim time," Liz called. She hurried over to me. She wore a pink one-piece bathing suit under crisp white tennis shorts.

I adjusted my swimsuit top. My hands were trembling.

I really was scared by what I planned to do.

"Why aren't you swimming?" Liz demanded. She brushed a fly off my shoulder.

"I — I don't have a buddy," I stammered.

She glanced around, trying to find someone for me. But everyone was in the lake.

"Well . . ." Liz twisted her mouth fretfully. "Go ahead and swim by yourself. Stay close to the shore. And I'll keep an eye on you."

"Great. Thanks," I said. I smiled at her, then trotted enthusiastically to the edge of the water.

I didn't want her to guess that it wasn't going to be a normal swim for me. That I had something really terrible in mind. . . .

I stepped into the water.

Oooh. So cold.

A cloud rolled over the sun. The sky darkened, and the air grew colder.

My feet sank into the muddy bottom of the lake. Up ahead, I saw the gnats — hundreds of them — hopping on the water.

Yuck, I thought. Why do I have to swim with mud and gnats?

I took a deep breath and stepped out farther. When the cold water was nearly up to my waist, I lowered my body in and started to swim.

I swam a few long laps. I needed to get used to the water. And I needed to get my breathing steady.

A short distance away, Briana and some other girls were having some kind of relay race. They were laughing and cheering. Having a great time.

They won't be laughing in a few minutes, I told myself bitterly.

A tall spray of water rushed over me. I cried out.

Another wave smacked my face.

It took me a few seconds to realize that I was being splashed — by Aaron.

He rose up in front of me — and spit a stream of water into my face.

"Yuck! How can you put this water in your mouth?" I cried, totally grossed out.

He laughed and splashed away to join his buddy.

He won't be laughing in a few minutes, either, I told myself. He'll treat me differently after today.

Everyone will.

I suddenly felt guilty. I should have told Aaron what I planned to do. I didn't really want to scare him. I wanted to scare everyone else.

But I knew if I told my plan to practical, sensible Aaron, he would talk me out of it. Or go tell Liz so that she would stop me.

Well . . . no one is going to stop me, I vowed.

Have you guessed my desperate plan?

It was really quite simple.

I planned to drown myself.

Well . . . not really.

I planned to dive down to the lake bottom. Stay under. A long, long time.

And make everyone think that I had drowned.

I can hold my breath for a very long time. It's because I play the flute. I've really developed my lung power.

I can probably stay underwater for two or three minutes.

Long enough to scare everyone to death.

Everyone will panic. Even Briana, Meg, and Jan.

Everyone will feel sorry for how mean they were to me.

I'll get a new start. After my close call in the lake, everyone in camp will want to be nice to me.

Everyone will want to be my buddy.

So . . . here goes.

I took one last look at all the laughing, shouting swimmers.

Then I sucked in the biggest breath I had ever taken.

And plunged down, down to the bottom of the lake.

14

The lake was shallow for only a few feet. Then the lake bottom gave way in a steep drop.

I kicked hard, pushing myself away from the other swimmers. Then I pulled myself upright, lowering my feet.

Yes.

I dropped my hands to my sides and let myself sink.

Down, down.

I opened my eyes as I dropped to the lake bottom. I saw only green. Waves of pale light shimmered through the green.

I'm floating inside an emerald, I thought. Floating down, down in a sparkling green jewel.

I pictured the tiny emerald on the ring Mom wore every day. Her engagement ring. I thought about Mom and Dad, thought how sad they'd be if I really did drown.

We never should have sent Sarah to that water sports camp, they would say.

My feet hit the soft lake floor.

A bubble of air escaped my mouth. I pressed my lips tighter, holding the air inside.

I slowly floated up toward the surface.

I closed my eyes. I kept my whole body still to make it look as if I'd drowned.

I pictured the horror on Liz's face when she saw my body floating so still, floating under the water, my hair bobbing on the surface.

I almost laughed when I thought of Liz leaping into the lake to rescue me, having to get her crisp white tennis shorts wet.

I forced myself to remain still.

I shut my eyes even tighter. And thought about Briana, Meg, and Jan.

They'll feel so guilty. They'll never forgive themselves for the way they treated me.

After my close call, they'll see how mean they were. And they'll want to be best friends with me.

We'll all be best friends.

And we'll have a great summer together.

My chest began to feel tight. The back of my throat began to burn.

I opened my lips and let out a few more bubbles of air.

But my throat still burned, and so did my chest.

I floated facedown. I kept my legs stiff and let my arms hang loosely at my sides.

I listened for shouts of alarm.

Someone must have spotted me by now.

I listened for cries of help. For kids calling Liz.

But I heard only silence. The heavy silence you hear when you're underwater.

I let out another bubble of air.

My chest really hurt now. It felt about to explode.

I opened my eyes. Was anyone nearby? Was anyone coming to rescue me?

I saw only green.

Where is everyone? I wondered.

Liz must have spotted me by now. Why isn't she pulling me up out of the water?

I pictured her again in her white tennis shorts. I pictured her tanned arms and legs. I pictured her red hair.

Liz — where are you?

Liz — don't you see me drowning here? You said you'd keep an eye on me, remember?

I can't stay under much longer.

My chest is ready to explode. My whole body is tingling. Burning. My head feels about to pop open.

Can't anyone see me here?

A wave of dizziness swept over me.

I shut my eyes, but the dizziness didn't go away.

I pushed out the rest of the air in my lungs.

No air, I thought. No air left. . . .

My arms and legs ached.

My chest burned.

With my eyes closed, I saw bright yellow spots.

Dancing yellow lights. They grew brighter . . . brighter. They did a fast, furious dance all around me.

Around my burning, tingling body.

My chest . . . exploding . . . exploding . . .

I'm so cold, I realized. Suddenly, I feel so cold.

The dancing, darting yellow lights grew brighter. Bright as spotlights. Bright as flashbulbs, flashing in my eyes.

Flashing around my still, cold body.

I shuddered from the cold.

Shuddered again.

Cold, thick water filled my mouth.

I've stayed under too long, I realized.

No one is coming. No one is coming to save me.

Too long . . . too long.

I struggled to see. But the lights were too bright.

Can't see. Can't see.

I swallowed another mouthful of water.

Can't see. Can't breathe.

I can't stay under any longer. I can't wait any longer.

I struggled to raise my head out of the water. But it felt so heavy. It weighed a ton.

Can't stay down . . .

Can't breathe.

With a burst of strength, I moved my shoulders. Pulled them up.

Hoisted up my head.

So heavy ... so heavy. My hair filled with water. My hair so heavy. The water running down my face.

Over my eyes.

I turned to shore. Squinted through the bright, darting lights.

Squinted hard through the water running down my face.

Squinted ...

No one there.

I turned again. My eyes searched the water.

No one there. No one swimming. No one on the shore.

Where is everyone? I wondered. Shivering. Shuddering.

Where did everyone go?

15

I struggled to shore.

My feet were numb. I couldn't feel the muddy bottom as I staggered out of the water.

I rubbed my arms. I couldn't feel the touch of my hands. Couldn't feel the water pouring off me, running down my back.

Couldn't feel anything. Numb. Numb all over.

"Where is everyone?" I called.

But did I make a sound? Did I have a voice?

I couldn't hear myself.

I stepped onto the grass and shook myself. Like a dog trying to get dry.

Trying to shake some feeling into my cold, numb body.

"Where did you all go?"

Hugging myself, I stumbled forward. I stopped when I saw the canoes. All tacked upside down by the shore and tied up.

Weren't kids canoeing today? Weren't the canoes all out in the lake?

"Hey!" I shouted.

But why couldn't I hear my shout?

"Where *is* everyone?"

No one on the shore.

I spun around, nearly losing my balance. No one in the water.

No one. No one anywhere.

I stumbled past the life preservers and rubber rafts. Covered with a canvas tarp.

Isn't anyone going to use them? I wondered. Why are they covered up?

Why did everyone leave the lake so quickly?

Shivering, hugging myself, I made my way toward the lodge. I gasped when I noticed the trees.

Bare. All winter bare.

"Noooooooo!" a frightened wail escaped my throat. A silent wail.

Could anyone hear me?

When had the leaves fallen? Why had they fallen in the middle of summer?

I started to trot along the path to the lodge. Cold. So cold.

Something stung my shoulder. Something tingled my eyelids.

Snow?

Yes. Tiny white flakes drifted down, blown by a steady breeze. The bare trees rattled and creaked.

I brushed snowflakes from my wet hair.

Snow?

But I knew that was impossible.

All impossible.

"Heeeeeeey!" My shout echoed through the trees. Or did it?

Could anyone hear my frightened call?

"Helllllllllp!" I shouted. "Somebody helllllp me!"

Silence, except for the creaking tree limbs overhead.

I started to run again. My bare feet moved silently over the cold ground.

The cabins came into view as I made my way out of the trees. Their flat roofs were covered by a thin layer of snow.

The ground was as gray as the sky. The cabins were all dark, the shingled walls gray. Gray all around me.

A cold world of gray.

I pushed open the door of the first cabin I came to. "Hey — I need help!" I cried.

I stared into the empty room.

No one there. No camp trunks. No clothes scattered about.

I raised my eyes to the bunk beds against the wall. The blankets, the sheets — the mattresses — had all been taken away.

I guess this cabin isn't being used, I thought.

I backed out of the door. Turned and ran down the row of cabins. All dark and silent.

My cabin stood where the path curved up the

hill. With a sigh of relief, I ran up to it and pushed open the door.

"Briana? Meg?"

Empty. And dark.

The mattresses gone. The posters pulled down. No clothes. No bags or trunks.

No sign that anyone had ever lived in here.

"Where *are* you?" I shrieked.

And then, "Where am *I*?"

Where was my stuff? Where was my bed?

Uttering another terrified wail, I lurched out of the cabin.

Cold. So cold and numb. Running through the cold in my wet bathing suit.

I tore through the camp. Pulling open doors. Peering into bare, empty rooms. Calling. Calling for someone — anyone — to help me.

Into the main lodge. My cries echoing off the high, wooden rafters.

Or did they? Was I really making a sound?

Why couldn't I hear myself?

I burst into the mess hall. The long, wooden benches had been stacked on top of the tables. The kitchen stood dark and empty.

What has happened? I wondered, unable to stop my trembling.

Where did everyone go? Why did they all leave? How did they leave so quickly? How can it be snowing?

I stumbled back out into the gray cold. Wisps of gray fog floated low over the gray ground. I hugged my frozen body, trying to warm myself.

Terrified and confused, I wandered from building to building. I felt as if I were swimming again. Swimming in the thick gray mists. Swimming through endless layers of gray.

And then I stopped when I heard a voice.

A tiny voice. A girl's voice.

Singing.

She was singing in a high, frail voice.

"I'm not alone!" I cried.

I listened to her song. A sad song sung so softly.

And then I called out to her, "Where are you? I can't see you! Where are you?"

16

I followed the tiny voice to the lodge. I saw a girl perched on the wooden steps.

"Hey!" I called. "Hey! I was looking for someone! Can you help me?"

She kept singing, as if she didn't see me. As I walked closer, I realized she was singing the Camp Cold Lake song in her tiny, light voice.

She had long curls of white-blond hair that flowed down the sides of her face. A pretty face, delicate and pale. So incredibly pale.

She wore a sleeveless white T-shirt and white short shorts. Snowflakes fell all around us. I shivered. But she didn't seem to notice the cold.

She tilted her head from side to side as she sang. Her round blue eyes stared out at the sky. They reminded me of shiny blue marbles in her pale, pale face.

I stepped up in front of her. I brushed snowflakes from my forehead.

She didn't turn to me until her song was finished. Then she smiled. "Hi, Sarah." Her speaking voice was as soft as her singing.

"How — how do you know my name?" I stammered.

Her smile grew wider. "I've been waiting for you," she replied. "My name is Della."

"Della — I'm so cold," I blurted out.

She rose to her feet. Turned. And pulled something out from behind the steps.

A white bathrobe.

She held it up and slipped it around my trembling shoulders.

Her hands were so light. I could barely feel them.

She helped me tie the belt. Then she stepped back and smiled at me again. "I've been waiting for you, Sarah," she said. Her voice was a sigh, a whisper.

"Excuse me?" I cried. "Waiting —?"

She nodded. Her white-blond hair fluttered with every move of her head. "I can't leave without you, Sarah. I need a buddy."

I stared at her, trying to understand.

"Where *is* everyone?" I cried. "Where did everyone go? Why are you the only one here?" I brushed snowflakes from my eyebrows. "Della, how did it get to be winter?"

"You'll be my buddy — won't you, Sarah?" Her blue eyes burned into mine. Her hair glowed around her pale face.

I blinked. "I don't understand —" I started. "Please answer my questions."

"You'll be my buddy, won't you?" she repeated, pleading with those amazing eyes. "I've waited so long for a buddy, Sarah. So long."

"But, Della —"

She started to sing again.

I shoved my hands into the pockets of the robe. I shivered. I couldn't get warm. I couldn't stop shaking.

Why was she singing the Camp Cold Lake song so sadly?

Why wouldn't she answer my questions?

How did she know my name? And why did she say she'd been waiting for me?

"Della, please —" I begged.

Singing her strange, sad song, she floated up the wooden stairs to the lodge. Her hair shimmered, golden in the gray light. Swirls of fog curled around her as she moved.

"Oh!" I cried out when I realized I could see right through her.

"Della —?"

She floated over the stairs, tilting her head from side to side, singing in that breathy whisper of a voice.

"Della —?"

She stopped singing and smiled at me again. Snowflakes covered her blond hair. The fog still swirled around her.

I could see the dark shingles of the lodge through her body. I stared right through her.

"Sarah, you're my buddy now," she whispered. "I need a buddy. Everyone at Camp Cold Lake needs a buddy."

"But — but *you're dead!*" I blurted out.

Della is dead, I realized.

And I'm her buddy.

That means . . .

That means *that I'm dead too*!

17

Della floated over me. So light and pale. The wind fluttered her hair. It rose around her like a shimmering halo.

"You're dead," I murmured. "And I am too."

Saying the words sent a cold shudder down my body.

I began to realize the truth. I began to see what had happened.

Della had probably drowned here. Drowned in the lake.

That is why everyone at the camp is so crazy about water safety.

That explains the endless water safety lectures. And the long list of rules. And why the counselors insist on the Buddy System at all times.

Della drowned here.

And now I'm her buddy.

I'm her buddy — because I drowned too.

"Noooooooooo!" A long wail of horror, of disbelief, escaped my throat.

I threw my head back and wailed like an animal. Wailed out my sorrow.

Della floated over me, watching me. Waiting for me to stop. She knew what I was thinking. She knew I had figured everything out.

She waited patiently. How long had she been waiting there for me? Waiting for a buddy? Another *dead* buddy?

How long had she been waiting for another unlucky girl to drown?

"Noooo!" I moaned. "No, I won't do it, Della! I can't do it! I won't be your buddy! I won't!"

I spun around. So dizzy, I nearly dropped to my knees.

I started to run. The white robe flew open. It flapped beside me like wings as I ran away from her.

Ran barefoot over the snowy ground.

Ran through the swirls of fog. Through the gray.

"Come back, Sarah!" I heard Della call to me. "Come back! You have to be my buddy! I'm trapped here. Trapped as a ghost. I can't leave this camp — I can't get to the other world — without a buddy!"

But I didn't stop. I kept running through the camp. Past the cabins. Past the supply sheds at the edge of the woods.

I kept running from her calls. Running from her ghostly voice.

I don't want to be her buddy, I told myself. I don't want to be a *ghost*!

I blinked away snowflakes as I ran. Ran through the bare, creaking trees. Ran without looking back.

I stopped when I reached the lake shore. Stopped when I felt the cold water lap over my feet.

The cold, gray water.

I struggled to catch my breath. But my chest hurt. Felt about to explode.

Gasping, I turned — and saw Della floating through the trees. Floating toward me, her eyes glowing with blue fire.

"You can't leave without me, Sarah!" she called. "You can't leave, Sarah!"

I turned away from her. Turned back to the water.

My chest. My head.

Everything hurt so much.

I couldn't breathe.

My chest was going to burst.

I sank to the mud.

As the gray faded to black.

18

Pinpricks of white light danced above me.

I thought of fireflies, darting above the grass late at night.

The tiny lights grew brighter. Round, like flashlight beams.

Brighter still.

Until I was staring into a glowing ball of gold.

I blinked.

It took me a long while to realize that I was staring up at the sun.

I turned my head away.

I suddenly felt heavy. I could feel the ground beneath me. I could feel the weight of my body on the ground.

My body. My solid body, coming back to me.

I heard a groan. Someone moved above me.

I blinked several times. And squinted up at Liz.

Her face was red. Her mouth was twisted in a hard scowl.

"Ohhh." I groaned as she pressed both hands on my chest. Raised her hands. Pressed again.

I felt water slide from my open mouth.

I choked. Felt more water pour down my chin.

"She's coming around," Liz announced. She pressed hard on my chest again. "She's alive!" Liz cried.

Behind her, I could see bare legs. Swimsuits. Campers.

Yes. The other campers.

I groaned again. Liz continued to work over me.

I'm lying on my back, I realized. I'm on the lake shore. Liz is giving me CPR.

The other campers are standing around me. Watching. Watching Liz save my life.

"I'm — ALIVE!" The word burst from my throat.

I sat up. And gazed around.

Everyone is back! I realized. It's summer again. The leaves are back on the trees. The sun is beaming down.

And everyone is back. Including me!

Liz uttered a sigh and sank back on her knees. "Sarah, are you okay?" she asked breathlessly. She mopped sweat from her forehead with the back of her hand. "Are you okay?"

"I . . . I think so," I murmured.

I had a sour taste in my mouth. I still felt a little dizzy.

Behind Liz, some campers cheered and applauded.

"We thought you were gone for a moment." Liz sighed. "You stopped breathing. What a scare!"

Two counselors helped me to my feet. I tried to shake off my dizziness. "I'm okay!" I cried. "Thank you, Liz. You — you saved my life!"

I hugged Liz. Then I turned and hugged Aaron.

Briana and Meg were standing nearby. I startled them by hugging them too.

I was so happy to be alive! So happy to be away from that gray, gray winter. Away from that frightening ghost girl in the empty camp.

"Sarah — what happened?" Liz asked, placing a hand on my still-wet shoulder. She gently brushed back my hair.

"I'm not sure," I told her. "I'm really not sure."

Liz shuddered. "When you stopped breathing, I . . . I got so scared."

"I'm fine now," I told her with a smile. "Thanks to you."

"She did it for attention," I heard someone mutter.

I turned — and saw Jan whispering to another girl. "Now everyone has to say 'Poor Sarah,'" Jan whispered nastily. "Now everyone has to be nice to her."

I felt hurt. I opened my mouth to say something to Jan.

70

But I was so happy to be back, so happy to be *alive*, I just ignored it.

I rested a hand on Aaron's shoulder and let him walk me back to my cabin. "I'm going to enjoy the rest of camp," I told my brother. "I really am."

The nurse checked me out carefully. Then I rested all afternoon. I took a long nap.

When I woke up, I was starving. I realized I hadn't eaten all day.

I pulled on jeans and a camp sweatshirt and hurried to the campfire. As I trotted down the path toward the clearing by the woods, the aroma of hot dogs and hamburgers on the barbecue drifted out to me.

Richard greeted me at the campfire circle. "Sarah, you look great!" he exclaimed. "I heard about . . . what happened at the lake this afternoon."

"Well, I'm fine now," I told him. "I feel great."

"Hey — no more close calls," he scolded. "Or else you have to swim in the kiddie pool."

"I'll be careful," I promised.

"You'd better — because we don't *have* a kiddie pool!" he joked.

I laughed.

"Take a seat," he said, pointing to the circle of logs. "Take a seat, everyone!" he called out. "We're going to have a meeting before we eat!"

Most of the campers had already taken their places. I glanced around the circle quickly, searching for a place to sit.

"Sarah —?" A voice called to me.

"Sarah — over here."

I let out a shocked cry when I saw Della.

Della. By herself on a log back near the woods. Her blond hair shimmering around her pale face. The pink evening sunlight shining through her body.

Shining right through her.

"Noooo!" I moaned.

"Come over here, Sarah!" Della called. "Please — sit over here with me. Be my buddy!"

19

I raised my hands to my cheeks and let out a shrill scream.

"No! You're not here!" I wailed. "You're a ghost! You don't belong here! I'm alive now! I'm alive!"

I turned and saw Richard and Liz hurrying toward me.

Across the circle, Aaron jumped up and came running over. "Sarah — what's wrong? What *is* it?" he cried.

"Don't you see her?" I shrieked. I pointed to the log near the woods. "She's a ghost! But I'm alive!"

Liz wrapped her arms around me. "It's okay, Sarah," she whispered. "You're okay now."

"But — but she's *sitting* there!" I sputtered.

Everyone turned to the log.

"There's no one there," Richard said. He narrowed his eyes at me.

"You had a terrible shock," Liz said softly. "A

terrible shock. You're still not quite yourself, Sarah."

"But — but —" I stammered.

I saw Briana, Meg, and Jan huddled together, talking softly. Watching me.

What are they saying about me? I wondered.

"Do you want me to walk you back to your cabin?" Richard asked.

I shook my head. "No. I'm starving!"

Liz laughed. "Maybe *that's* your problem. You're so hungry, you're seeing things! Let's get you a hot dog — fast."

After a couple of hot dogs, I started to feel better. The campfire meeting began. I sat next to some girls from a different cabin.

As Richard talked, I gazed around the circle. Stared at the campers' faces, orange from the flickering campfire. Searching for Della.

Della the ghost . . .

Was she still here? Still watching me? Still waiting for me to be her buddy?

I sat forward tensely. My whole body stiff. My eyes straining to see her pale, pale face.

But she had vanished.

For now.

Liz took over the meeting. Most campers groaned when she started another lecture on water safety.

"We had a close call today," Liz said. "A frightening close call."

I knew everyone was staring at me. I could feel my face growing hot. I gazed into the yellow flames of the campfire.

When I raised my eyes, I saw Briana, Meg, and Jan on the next log, whispering together. About me?

"Our water safety rules are so important here at Camp Cold Lake," Liz was saying. "Some campers joke that having so many rules is the *curse* of Camp Cold Lake, because we talk about the rules so much."

She pressed her hands against her sides. Her eyes moved from camper to camper. "But as we saw this afternoon," she continued, "the Buddy System isn't a curse — it's a blessing."

A face rose up behind the darting flames of the fire.

I gasped.

Della!

No. A girl from another cabin, climbing up to get more food.

I sank back.

I have to get *away* from this camp, I decided. I can't have a good time here. Not if I always have to keep an eye out for Della.

Liz rattled on about the water rules.

Richard made a few announcements.

Everyone sang some camp songs.

When the campfire ended, I jumped up quickly and started along the path to my cabin. I had gone

75

only a few steps when I heard fast footsteps behind me. And heard someone calling my name.

Was it the ghost?

I turned to see Aaron jogging up to me. "What was that screaming about?" he demanded. "Did you *really* think you saw a ghost?"

"Why should I tell you?" I snapped. I continued along the path, walking rapidly. "You'll only laugh at me."

"Try me," he replied, running to catch up. "I won't laugh. I promise."

"I saw a ghost girl," I told him. "I swear I did. She called to me. She wants me to be her buddy."

Aaron laughed. "No. Really," he said. "What did you *really* see? Be serious."

"I *am* serious!" I cried. "I have to get away from here, Aaron. I'm going to run away. Get to a phone. Call Mom and Dad. Tonight. I'm going to tell them to come get me."

"You can't!" Aaron replied. He grabbed my arm and forced me to stop walking. I could see kids staring at us as they walked past.

"Mom and Dad won't want to make more than one trip up here. So if you call them, they'll make *me* come home too," Aaron protested. "And I don't want to leave. I'm having a great time!"

"You don't understand," I told him. "I can't stay here. I can't —"

"Please, Sarah," he begged. "Try to stick it out. Give it a little more time. You're just a little messed up because of the lake this afternoon. But you'll be okay. Give it some time."

I didn't say yes, and I didn't say no.

I just told Aaron good-night and headed to my cabin.

I stopped outside the door. All the lights were on. I heard Briana, Meg, and Jan talking softly.

They stopped talking as soon as I stepped inside.

All three of them stared hard at me. Their expressions were tense. They moved quickly.

Moved toward me as I started across the room.

They formed a circle around me. Surrounded me.

"What *is* it?" I cried. "What are you going to do?"

20

"We want to apologize," Briana said.

"We've been kind of rough on you," Jan added in her scratchy voice. "We're really sorry."

"We've been talking about it," Briana said. "We —"

"We decided we've been really unfair," Meg interrupted. "We're sorry, Sarah."

"I — I'm sorry too," I stammered. I was so stunned by their apologies, I could barely speak.

"Let's start all over," Briana suggested. She grabbed my hand. "Nice to meet you, Sarah. My name is Briana."

"Excellent. A fresh start!" Jan declared.

"Thanks. I'm really glad," I told them. And I meant it.

Jan turned to Briana. "When did you do that to your nails?"

Briana grinned and raised both hands. Her fingernails were a shiny, bright purple. "It's a new color," she said. "I did it after our swim."

"What color is it?" Meg asked.

"Grape Juice, I think," Briana replied. "They all have such crazy names." She dug the bottle of nail polish from her pack and held it out to me. "Want to try it?"

"Well . . . *sure*," I replied.

All four of us stayed up far past Lights Out, making our fingernails purple.

Later, I lay in my bunk, drifting off to sleep. I had a smile on my face, thinking about my three bunk mates. My three *friends*.

They had really cheered me up.

But my smile faded when I heard a whispered voice float across the dark cabin. "Sarah . . . Sarah . . ."

I gasped.

And then the frail voice — soft as the wind — was so close . . . so close to my ear.

"Sarah. I thought you were my buddy, Sarah. Why did you leave me?"

"No — please —" I begged.

"Sarah, I waited so long for you," the ghostly voice whispered. "Come with me. Come with me, Sarah. . . ."

And then an icy hand gripped my shoulder.

21

"Ohhhhh!"

I bolted up in the bunk. And stared out at Briana's dark eyes.

She let go of my shoulder. "Sarah," she whispered. "You were whimpering in your sleep."

"Huh? What?" My voice quivered. My heart pounded. I realized I was drenched in sweat.

"You were whimpering in your sleep," Briana repeated. "Crying and moaning. I thought I'd better wake you."

"Uh . . . thanks," I choked out. "Must have been a bad dream, I guess."

Briana nodded and crept back to her bunk.

I didn't move. I sat there trembling, staring out across the dark cabin.

A bad dream?

I didn't think so. . . .

"You can skip the long-distance swim today if you want," Liz told me at breakfast the next morning. She leaned over my chair as I downed my cornflakes. I could smell the toothpaste on her breath.

"Well . . ." I hesitated. "How long is the swim?"

"We're swimming halfway across the lake," Liz replied. "Halfway out, then back. I'll be in a boat at the halfway point. It isn't really that far. But if you feel like skipping it today . . ."

I set down my spoon. I could see Meg and Briana watching me from across the table. Beside me, Jan was struggling to choke down a half-toasted, frozen waffle.

"Come on. Swim with us," Briana urged.

"I'll be your buddy," Jan said. "I'll swim with you, Sarah."

Our frightening canoe adventure flashed into my mind. Once again, I pictured that horrible moment when Jan jumped from the canoe. Tipping it over. Leaving me there.

But things were different now.

We were friends. All four of us were friends now. I had to forget about what happened with the canoe. I had to forget about our bad start.

"Okay," I agreed. "Thanks, Jan. I'll be your buddy." I turned back to Liz. "I'm ready to swim."

The morning sun still floated low in the sky. It kept fading behind broad, gray clouds. And each time the sun disappeared, the air became as cold as the water.

The lake was so cold in the early morning!

As I waded in, I suddenly realized why it was named "Cold Lake."

We all stepped carefully into the water, shivering and complaining. The water lapped over my ankles, stinging them. I stopped with a gasp and waited to get used to the cold.

I raised my eyes at the sound of a motorboat and saw Liz chugging to her place in the middle of the lake. When she reached the spot, she cut the engine. Then she picked up an electric megaphone.

"Warm up first, everyone!" she instructed us.

We all laughed. "Warm up? How are we supposed to warm up? It's freezing!"

Two girls near the shore began splashing each other.

"Stop it! Whoooa! It's *collld*!" one of them shrieked.

Taking another few steps over the soft lake bottom, I adjusted the top of my blue swimsuit. "We need wet suits," I told Jan.

She nodded, then waded out until the water lapped at her waist. "Come on, Sarah. Stick together." She motioned for me to follow.

I took a deep breath — and plunged into the water.

A shock of cold swept over my body. But I dove under the water and swam out a few strokes. Then I raised my head and turned back to Jan.

"Show off," she muttered. She dipped her hands in the water, still struggling to get used to the cold.

I laughed. "It's refreshing!" I exclaimed, brushing my wet hair back. "Come on — just push off. It isn't that bad."

Jan lowered herself into the water. Most of the swimmers were in the water now, moving in circles, floating on their backs, treading water.

"Line up, everyone!" Liz instructed from her boat. Her voice through the megaphone echoed off the trees behind us. "Line up. Two at a time. Let's go!"

It took a while for everyone to get in place. Jan and I were second in line.

I watched the first two girls begin to swim. One of them moved with smooth, steady strokes. The other one splashed and thrashed.

Everyone cheered them on.

Jan and I gave them about a two-minute head start. Then we began to swim.

I tried to copy the first girl's rhythmic stroke. I didn't want to look like a klutz. I knew all the other swimmers were watching. But let's get real. I'm not exactly headed for the Olympics.

Jan pulled ahead easily. As we swam, she kept turning back to make sure I was keeping up with her.

The turnaround spot was just past Liz's motorboat. I kept my eyes on it as I followed Jan through the water. It seemed *very* far away!

Jan picked up speed. My arms started aching about halfway to the boat.

I'm in bad shape, I told myself. I've really got to start working out or something.

Liz's boat bobbed gently up ahead of us. Liz was shouting something into the megaphone. But the splash of the water kept me from making out the words.

Up ahead of me, Jan picked up the pace.

"Hey — slow down!" I called. But there was no way she could hear me.

Ignoring the aching in my arms, I struggled to catch up to her. I kicked my legs harder, splashing up water behind me.

The sun dipped once again behind a high cloud. The sky darkened, and the water seemed to chill.

Liz's boat rocked in the water, just up ahead. I kept my eyes on Jan. Watched her steady kicks. Her hair bobbing on the lake surface like some kind of sea creature.

When Jan turns back, I'll turn back, I decided.

I swam a little faster. *Let's turn*, I pleaded silently. Jan, we're here. We're even with Liz's motorboat. I'm ready to turn back now.

But to my surprise, Jan kept stroking, kept swimming straight ahead. Her head ducked under the water. Her arms moved easily, gracefully, pulling her farther ahead of me.

"Jan —?"

My arms ached. My chest started to burn.

84

"Hey, Jan — can we turn now?"

She swam steadily ahead.

With a burst of energy, I pulled myself forward. "Jan, wait —" I called. "We're supposed to head back!"

She stopped stroking.

Did she hear me?

Breathing hard, my chest burning, I swam up to her.

She turned to face me.

"Jan —?" I gasped.

No. Not Jan.

It wasn't Jan. *It was Della!*

Her blue eyes sparkled as a gleeful smile spread over her pale, pale face.

"Keep swimming, Sarah," she whispered. "We're going to swim farther. And farther. You're my buddy now."

22

She grabbed my arm.

I tried to tug away. My wet arm slid in her grasp.

But her grip tightened around my wrist. And she held on. Pulling me. Pulling me with her.

"Owww!"

She was strong. So strong for such a frail-looking girl.

Such a frail-looking *ghost* . . .

"Let go!" I shrieked.

I struggled, slapping the water. Kicking. Squirming and twisting.

"Della — I won't come with you!"

I jerked my body around, spun hard — and broke free.

And dropped beneath the surface. Lifting both arms, I rose up, coughing and sputtering.

Where was she?

Where?

Was she right behind me? Ready to pull me with her, pull me out so far I couldn't swim back?

I spun away. The water rocked and tilted.

The clouds overhead appeared to roar past.

"Sarah ... Sarah ...?" Was she calling to me?

Why couldn't I see her now?

I turned again. My eyes stopped on the boat.

Yes. The boat.

Ignoring my racing heartbeats, my aching arms, I plunged forward.

The boat ... got to reach the boat before she grabs me again.

Swimming furiously, kicking with my last bit of strength, I dove for the boat. Stretching my arms out ... stretching ...

And grabbed the side with both hands. Choking and gasping.

Grabbed the side of the boat and tried to pull myself in.

"Liz — help me." The words escaped my throat in a hoarse whisper.

"Liz — help me in."

The sun burst out from behind the clouds. I stared up into blinding golden light.

"Liz — please ..."

Hands reached down for me. She bent to pull me into the motorboat.

Leaned forward. Pulling me up.

Blinking against the bright sunlight, I raised my eyes to her face.

No!

Not Liz's face. Not Liz!

Della!

Della — pulling me into the boat.

"What's wrong, Sarah?" she whispered. Pulling me. Pulling me up to her.

"Sarah, you're okay. You're perfectly okay."

23

"Let go!" I wailed.

I tore myself from her grip.

And tried to blink away the sun.

And stared up at Liz.

Not Della. Liz. Her face twisted in concern.

"Sarah, you're okay," she repeated.

"But —" I stared up at her. Waiting for her face to change again. Waiting for her to become Della again.

Had I only imagined Della's face? Had the streaming sunlight tricked my eyes?

With a sigh, I let her help me into the boat.

I slumped to my knees. The boat rocked up and down. Liz narrowed her eyes at me. "What happened out there?" she asked.

Before I could answer, I heard splashing outside the boat.

Della?

I froze.

No. Jan pulled herself up on the side. She

brushed her wet hair off her face. "Sarah — didn't you hear me calling you?" she demanded.

"Jan. I didn't see you. I thought that —" My voice caught in my throat.

"Why did you swim away from me?" Jan asked. "I'm your buddy — remember?"

Liz drove me to shore. I changed my clothes and went to see Richard. I found him in his head counselor's office, a little room about the size of a closet in the back of the main lodge.

He was resting his feet on top of his tiny desk. He twirled a toothpick in his mouth.

"Hey, Sarah — how's it going?" He flashed me a friendly smile and motioned for me to take a seat in the folding chair across from his desk.

I could see his eyes studying me.

"I hear you had another little problem in the lake," he said softly. He moved the toothpick to the other side of his mouth. "What's going on?"

I took a deep breath.

Should I tell him there is a ghost girl who has been following me everywhere? Who wants me to be her buddy?

He'd just think I'm nuts, I decided.

"You had a bad shock yesterday," Richard said. "We really thought that you drowned."

He lowered his feet and leaned over the desk toward me. "Maybe you went back in the water too soon," he said. "Too soon after the shock."

"Maybe," I murmured.

And then I blurted out the question that was really on my mind. "Richard, tell me about the girl who drowned here."

His mouth dropped open. "Huh?" The toothpick fell onto his lap.

"I know that a girl drowned in the lake," I insisted. "Can you tell me about her?"

Richard shook his head. "No girl ever drowned at Camp Cold Lake," he said. "Never."

I knew he was lying.

I had proof, after all. I had seen Della. And talked with her.

"Richard, please —" I begged. "I really need to know. Tell me about her."

He frowned. "Why don't you believe me, Sarah? I'm telling the truth. No campers have ever drowned at this camp. No boys. No girls."

I heard a soft sigh behind me.

I glanced back at the open doorway — and saw Della standing there.

I jumped to my feet. And pointed. "Richard!" I cried. "The girl who drowned! She's standing right there! Don't you see her?"

Richard raised his eyes to the doorway. "Yes," he replied softly. "I see her."

24

"Huh?" I gasped and grabbed the edge of his desk. "You see her?" I cried. "You really do?"

Richard nodded. He had a solemn expression on his face. "If it makes you feel better, Sarah, I'll say that I see her."

"But you don't *really* see her?" I demanded.

He scratched his sandy-colored hair. "No. I don't see anything."

I turned back to the doorway. Della grinned at me.

"Sit down. Please," Richard instructed. "You know, sometimes our mind plays tricks on us. Especially when we've been through a really bad scare."

I didn't sit down. I stood in front of his desk and stared hard at Della. Stared right through her.

"She's not in my mind! She's right there!" I shouted. "She's standing right there, Richard. Her name is Della. She drowned at this camp. And now she's trying to drown me too!"

"Sarah — please calm down," Richard said gently. He climbed around his desk and put a hand on my shoulder. Then he led me to the door.

I was standing face-to-face with Della.

She stuck out her tongue at me.

"See? There's no one there," Richard said.

"But — but —" I sputtered.

"Why don't you stay away from the lake for a few days," he suggested. "You know. Just hang out and relax."

Della mouthed his words as he spoke.

I turned away from her.

She giggled.

"Don't go to the lake?" I asked Richard.

He nodded. "Take a few days and rest up. You'll feel much better."

I knew I wouldn't feel better. I knew I'd still have Della following me everywhere, trying to make me her buddy.

I sighed. "That won't help," I told him.

"Then I have a different idea," he said. "Pick a sport you haven't tried, Sarah. Pick something really hard. Like water-skiing."

"I don't get it," I replied. "Why should I do that?"

"Because you will have to think so hard about what you're doing, you won't have time to worry about ghosts."

I rolled my eyes. "Yeah. Right."

"I'm *trying* to help you," he said sharply.

"Well . . . thanks," I replied. I didn't know what else to say. "I guess I'll go to lunch now."

I trudged out of the tiny office. And took a deep breath. The air was much cooler out in the main lodge.

I turned the corner and headed toward the mess hall in the front of the building. As I turned another corner, I heard Della's frail voice behind me.

"You can't get away, Sarah. You're my buddy. There's no need to run. You'll *always* be my buddy."

The soft words — so close to my ear — sent shivers down my back.

Something inside me snapped.

I couldn't hold in my fury.

"SHUT UP!" I shrieked. "SHUT UP! SHUT UP! SHUT UP — AND LEAVE ME ALONE!"

I spun around to see if she had heard me.

And gasped in horror.

25

Briana stood behind me.

Her mouth dropped open in shock. "Okay, okay. I'll go away," she said, backing up. "You don't have to be so nasty, Sarah. I was just coming to see how you were doing."

Wow. I felt so bad.

Briana thought I was talking to her.

"I — I —" I stammered.

"I thought you wanted to be friends," Briana snapped. "I didn't even say a word to you. And you bit my head off!"

"I wasn't talking to you!" I finally choked out. "I was talking to *her*!"

I pointed to Della, who leaned against the wall behind us. Della waved to me and giggled.

Sun from the open lodge window lit up Della's blond hair from behind. I could see the window right through her body.

"I was talking to her!" I repeated.

Briana raised her eyes to the window.

And the *strangest* expression spread over her face.

The next morning, I gulped down some gooey scrambled eggs for breakfast. Then I made my way to the boat dock.

Don't ask why I decided to try water-skiing.

I really don't have an answer.

I suppose I did it for Aaron. The night before, he begged me once again not to call Mom and Dad.

Aaron really didn't want to go home. He said he was having the best summer of his life.

Sure, I thought. It's *easy* for you to have a good summer. You don't have a ghost following you around.

"Please try to stay a while longer," Aaron begged.

I won't go to the lake, I decided. I'll hang around the cabin and read or something.

But in the morning, I realized that was a bad plan.

I'd be too scared to stay by myself in the cabin while everyone else was at the lake. I would have no way to protect myself against Della.

Yes, I know I wasn't thinking clearly.

I was so stressed out, I could barely think at all!

I should have stayed as far away from the water as possible.

But I really didn't want to be alone. So I followed

Richard's advice. And went to the boat dock. And told Liz I wanted to try water-skiing.

"That's great, Sarah!" Liz cried, flashing me a pleased smile. "Have you ever done it before? It's easier than it looks."

I told her I'd never tried it.

She pulled a yellow inflated life vest and a pair of skis from the equipment shed.

Then she gave me a short lesson. Showed me how to lean back and how to bend my knees.

A short while later, I was in the water waiting for the motorboat to come around. Meg was using the boat now, skiing behind it, sliding over the water. Her orange bathing suit glowed in the morning sunlight.

The hum of the boat echoed over the water. The lake bobbed and rippled in the boat's wake.

Meg let out a cry and let go of the towrope as the boat sped near the dock. She splashed into the water, then quickly pulled off her skis. Then she came walking to shore.

"My turn next," I said softly. I felt a knot in my stomach.

Meg flashed me a thumbs-up.

I struggled with the skis, but finally got them in place. Then I pulled up the towrope, gripping it tightly in both hands.

The boat motor sputtered and coughed. The boat rocked up ahead of me in the rippling blue water.

I steadied myself. Lowered myself the way Liz had shown me. And took a deep breath.

"Ready!" I called.

The motor sputtered — and then roared.

The boat pulled away so fast, the towrope nearly flew out of my hands.

"Whooooooooaaa!" I opened my mouth in a long cry as the rope pulled me up.

Yes! The skis bounced over the surface. I bent my knees and gripped the towrope tightly.

I'm doing it! I realized. I'm water-skiing!

The boat picked up speed. We headed in a straight line over the sparkling water. The cold spray swept over my face, my hair.

I started to lose my balance. Tugged myself back up. Held on — and kept going.

"Yessss!" I cried out loud. What an awesome feeling!

But then the driver of the boat turned her head.

And I recognized Della's evil grin.

As she worked the controls, Della's white-blond hair flew up like wings around her pale face. Her blue eyes sparkled like the water.

Her grin grew wider as she saw the horror on my face.

"Turn around! Turn back! Please!" I begged.

She made the boat swerve hard.

I nearly toppled over. I gripped the towrope.

My skis slapped the surface. Pain shot up to my knees. The cold spray washed over me.

I gasped. Struggled to breathe.

Della threw back her head and laughed. The sound was drowned out by the roar of the motor.

I could see the sky through her body. The sunlight poured right through her.

"Turn around!" I screamed. "Stop! Where are you taking me? *Where?*"

26

Della didn't answer. She turned away from me, her hair flying wildly behind her head.

The boat bounced over the water, sending up tall waves of foam and spray.

The waves splashed over me. Chilling me. Blinding me.

Gripped in panic, it took me a long time to realize that I had an easy escape.

I let go of the towrope.

My hands shot up. The tow bar snapped against the water.

I skidded for a few seconds, my arms thrashing wildly. And then I toppled over and sank.

The life vest pulled me back up. I bounced on the surface, gasping, spitting out water. My heart pounded.

I felt so dizzy. The bright sunlight seemed to surround me. Which way was up? Which way to the shore?

I spun around and saw the motorboat in the distance.

"You didn't get me *this* time!" I called to Della.

But then I froze as the boat began to turn. Della swerved the boat, kicking up a tall wave of white water.

Swerved it back around. Until it pointed to me.

I gasped as I heard the motor roar.

I bobbed helplessly in the water.

The boat picked up speed, skipping over the rippling surface.

She's coming for me, I thought. She's coming to make me her buddy forever.

I'm trapped out here.

She's coming to run me over.

27

I treaded water, watching in horror as the boat sped toward me.

I've got to dive under it, I realized. The only way to escape is *down*.

I took a deep breath. Every muscle tensed. I knew I had to time my dive perfectly.

The boat roared closer. I could see Della crouched over the motor. Guiding the boat.

Aiming it.

I took another deep breath. And then I realized I couldn't dive.

The life vest — it was holding me up. No way I could plunge beneath the surface.

With a cry, I grabbed the front of the vest with both hands.

And tugged.

I can't do this! I realized. *I can't get this thing off in time!*

The water rocked harder as the boat sped nearer. The whole lake seemed to tilt and spin.

102

The boat — it's going to tear me to pieces! I thought.

I pulled at the vest. Pushed it.

Please — please — slide over my head!

No time. No time.

I can't dive!

The motor's roar drowned out my scream.

With a frantic tug, I pulled the life vest up. Over my shoulders.

Too late.

The front of the boat bounced over me.

Then the whirring motor blades sliced off my head.

28

I waited for the pain.

I waited for the darkness.

The water swirled around me. Blue, then green.

Choking on a mouthful of water, I thrashed up to the surface. Struggling to breathe, I let the waves rock me back and forth.

"The life vest!" I choked out.

I held half of the vest in each hand.

The motor blades had sliced the life vest in two.

I tossed the two pieces away. And started to laugh.

"I'm alive!" I cried out loud. "I'm still alive!"

I turned and saw the boat speeding across the lake. Did Della think she had won?

I didn't care. I spun around. Found the shore. And started to swim.

My close call gave me new energy. The strong, rocking current helped push me back to the camp.

I heard girls calling to me as I stumbled onto the grass. And I saw Liz jogging quickly over.

"Sarah —" she called. "Sarah — wait!"

I ignored her. I ignored them all.

I started to run.

I knew what I had to do. I had to get away from Camp Cold Lake. I had to get away as fast as I could.

I wasn't safe here. Not as long as Della wanted me for her buddy. Not as long as Della wanted me to drown too.

I knew no one would believe me. They all said they wanted to help. But no one could really help me — not against a ghost!

I burst into the cabin and tore off my wet swimsuit. Tossing it to the floor, I frantically pulled on shorts and a T-shirt.

I swept my wet hair back with both hands. Tugged on socks and my sneakers.

"Got to get away. Got to get away," I chanted to myself.

What to do? Where to go?

I'll run through the woods to the town on the other side, I decided. I'll call Mom and Dad. I'll tell them I'm hiding in town. I'll tell them to pick me up there.

I stopped at the cabin doorway.

Should I tell Aaron?

No. No way, I decided.

He'll only try to stop me.

I'll get a message to Aaron from town, I decided. I'll tell him where I am. But not until I'm safe. Not until I'm far away from this place.

I poked my head out of the cabin and searched around, making sure the coast was clear. Then I stepped outside and made my way around to the back.

And ran into Briana.

She narrowed her eyes at me, studying my face. "You're going?" she asked quietly.

I nodded. "Yes. I'm going."

Once again, Briana's expression changed. The light in her eyes seemed to fade.

"Good luck," she whispered.

29

Why is *she* acting so weird? I wondered.

I didn't have time to think about it. I gave Briana a wave. Then I ran past her and headed into the woods.

I glanced back as I followed a path between the trees. And saw Briana still standing there behind the cabin. Watching me.

Taking a deep breath, I turned and hurried along the path.

The trees overhead cut off a lot of the sunlight. It grew darker and cooler as I ran.

A hedge of sharp burrs and brambles scraped my bare arms and legs as I tried to edge past. I wished I had worn jeans and a sweatshirt. Something that covered me better.

My sneakers slipped over a thick blanket of dead leaves. I had to skip over fallen tree limbs and clumps of thorny weeds.

Tree roots rose up over the path. Tall, dry reeds leaned over me, as if reaching to grab me.

The narrow path divided in two. I paused — breathing hard — trying to decide which path to take.

Would they both lead me to town?

I held my breath when I heard a voice. Singing. A bird?

No. A soft voice. A girl's voice.

"Oh, no," I moaned. Raising my eyes to the sound, I saw Della, perched on a low tree limb. She tilted her head from side to side as she sang. Her blue eyes sparkled, gazing down at me.

"You — you followed me!" I stammered. "How did you know that I —" My voice caught in my throat.

She giggled. "You're my buddy," she replied. "We have to stick together."

"No! No way!" I screamed up at her. "You lose, Della. I'm not going to be your buddy. Because I'm never going to the lake again. I'm never going to drown like you!"

Della's smile faded. "Drown?" She shook her head. "Sarah, what made you think that? You're very confused. I didn't drown."

"Huh?" My mouth dropped open. I stared up at her in shock.

"Close your mouth, Sarah. A fly will fly into it." Della tilted back her head and laughed.

Then she shook her head again. "How could *anyone* drown at Camp Cold Lake?" she demanded. "They give a lecture about water safety every five minutes! No one ever drowned at Camp Cold Lake!"

"You didn't drown?" I cried. "Then how did you die?"

She rested her hands on the tree limb and leaned forward, peering down at me. I could see through her body, see the leaves shaking in the breeze.

"It's a simple story," Della said with a sigh. "One night I got tired of listening to the water safety lecture at the campfire. So I sneaked off into these woods."

She swept her hair back with a toss of her head. "I made one major mistake," she continued. "I didn't know the woods are filled with deadly poisonous snakes."

I gasped. "These woods? Snakes?"

Della nodded. "It's nearly impossible to cross through these woods without getting bitten," she sighed. "I died of a snakebite, Sarah."

"But — but —" I sputtered. "But you were always at the lake," I choked out. "Why did I always see you at the lake?"

"Don't you get it?" she replied. "That was my plan. I made you afraid of the lake, Sarah. I made you *terrified* of the lake. Because I knew you'd try to escape through the woods. I knew you'd run into the woods and die like me — and be my buddy."

"No —!" I protested. "I won't. I —"

"Sarah, look!" Della pointed toward the ground.

I gazed down — and watched a fat black snake curl around my leg.

30

"Buddies forever," Della sang cheerfully. "Buddies forever."

I stood frozen, gaping down in horror. Watching the fat snake wind itself around me. Feeling its warm, dry body scrape over my bare skin.

"Nooooo." A low moan escaped my throat as the snake arched its head.

"It won't hurt that much," Della said brightly. "It's like a bee sting, Sarah. That's all."

The snake let out a loud hiss. It snapped open its jaws.

I felt its body tighten like a warm rope around my leg.

"Buddies forever," Della sang. "Buddies forever . . ."

"No! Sarah is *not* your buddy!" a voice rang out.

I tried to turn toward the voice. But I couldn't move. I felt the snake tighten its hold on my leg.

"Briana!" I cried. "What are *you* doing here?"

She hurried out from behind a clump of tall reeds.

With one quick motion, she grabbed the snake in one hand. Slid it off my leg. And tossed it into the trees.

Briana raised her eyes to Della. "Sarah can't be your buddy, because she's *my* buddy!" Briana shouted.

Della's eyes grew wide. She cried out in surprise. She gripped the tree branch to keep from falling.

"You!" she exclaimed. "What are *you* doing here?"

"Yes, it's me!" Briana shouted up to her. "I'm back, Della."

"But — but how did you . . ." Della's voice trailed off.

"You tried to do the same thing to me last year," Briana said. "You tried all summer to make *me* your buddy. You terrified me — didn't you, Della?"

Briana uttered an angry cry. "You didn't think I'd come back. But I did. I came back to camp this summer . . . to protect the next girl!"

"Nooo!" Della wailed.

I finally understood. I stepped up to the tree beside Briana. "Briana is my buddy!" I declared. "And I'm coming back next summer to warn the *next* girl!"

"No! No! Nooooo!" Della raged. "You can't do that! I've waited so long! So lonnnng!"

She let go of the tree limb and shook her fists at Briana and me.

Lost her balance.

Her hands flew up as she started to fall.

She grabbed for the limb. Missed.

And dropped silently to the ground.

Then she was gone.

Vanished.

With a weary sigh, I climbed to my feet. I shook my head. "Is she gone for good?" I murmured.

Briana shrugged. "I don't know. I hope so."

I turned to Briana. "You — you saved my life!" I cried. "Thank you for following me. Thank you for saving me!"

With a happy cry, I stepped up to her. "Thank you! Thank you!"

I wrapped my arms around her to hug her.

And my hands went right through her body.

I gasped. I grabbed her shoulder. But I couldn't feel a thing.

I jumped back in shock.

Briana narrowed her eyes at me. "Della killed me last summer, Sarah," she said softly. "On the last day. But I didn't want to be her buddy. I just never liked her."

She floated forward, raised herself off the ground, hovered over me.

"But I need a buddy," she whispered. "Everyone has to have a buddy. You'll be my buddy — won't you, Sarah?"

I saw the hissing snake in her hand.

But I couldn't move.

"You'll be my buddy — won't you?" Briana repeated. "You'll be my buddy forever."

About R.L. Stine

R.L. Stine is the most popular author in America. He is the creator of the *Goosebumps*, *Give Yourself Goosebumps*, *Fear Street*, and *Ghosts of Fear Street* series, among other popular books. He has written more than 100 scary novels for kids. Bob lives in New York City with his wife, Jane, teenage son, Matt, and dog, Nadine.

Add *more*

Goosebumps ®

to your collection . . .
A chilling preview of
what's next from
R.L. STINE

MY BEST FRIEND
IS INVISIBLE

4

I propped up my pillows and picked up the ghost-story book I was reading. I stared down at the page, but it was all just a blur.

I closed the book and drifted off to sleep. But I tossed and turned all night long. Half asleep, half awake, I fluffed up my pillow. I pulled the covers up around me. I drifted off again — then woke up to a noise.

Flapping.

The flapping of my curtains in the night breeze.

I sat up. I rubbed my eyes.

I stared at the window.

The *open* window!

I bolted out of bed and slammed it shut.

Who opened this window? WHO?

Is it possible for a window to slide *up*?

NO.

It must be Simon. Simon must be playing a joke on me, I decided.

But it couldn't be Simon. Simon doesn't play jokes. He's always serious.

I climbed back in bed — and stared at the window. Watching. Waiting. Waiting to see it open.

But my eyelids grew heavy and I fell asleep.

The next morning I woke up late. Brutus always wakes me up. But he didn't today.

I bolted up in bed to check the window. Closed.

I glanced at my desk chair. Brutus was gone.

I dressed quickly. I caught my reflection in the mirror as I headed out of my room. I looked wrecked.

"Sammy, you look awful," Mom said. "Did you get to bed late last night?"

I slumped down at the kitchen table. Dad sat across from me, reading the newspaper.

"No, not too late," I told Mom.

Dad peered over the newspaper. "You're reading too many of those ghost books, Sammy. If you read about real science, you'd sleep better."

Dad went back to his newspaper.

Mom poured some cereal into my breakfast bowl. I ate one spoonful — and Simon called me.

"Sammy — come up here," he shouted from his bedroom. "I need your help."

I ignored him.

I ate another spoonful.

"SAM-MY!" he screamed.

"Sammy, go see what your brother wants," Mom ordered.

"SAM-MY! SAM-MY!"

"WHAT?" I cried, charging into his room. "What's your problem?"

"*That!*" he said, pointing to the bed. "That is my problem."

Brutus lay curled up in Simon's bed.

"He slept in here last night," Simon said. "And now I can't get him out. He won't move."

"Brutus slept in here?"

I couldn't believe it.

Brutus always sleeps in my room. Always.

"Yes, he slept in here," Sammy said. "And I want him out!"

"What's the big deal? Just leave him there." I turned to the door.

"Wait!" Simon yelled. "I can't leave him there. I can't!"

"Why not?" I asked, confused.

"Because I have to make my bed," Simon answered.

I stared hard at my brother. "What planet are you from?"

"Sammy," Simon whined. "I have to make my bed. Mom says."

"Just make the bed over him. Mom won't notice the lump."

I returned to the kitchen a few seconds later. I sat down at the table.

Mom peered over my shoulder. "Sammy, how did you finish your cereal so fast?"

"Huh?"

I stared down into my breakfast bowl.

Totally empty!

5

"Someone — someone ate my cereal!" I stammered.

"You're right!" Mom gasped. "It must have been a ghost!"

Mom and Dad laughed.

I stared at the empty bowl — and the spoon.

"Look!" I shouted. "Someone *did* eat my cereal. I have proof! The spoon — it's on the left side of the bowl. I always put my spoon on the right side of the bowl — because I'm right-handed. See?"

I pointed to the spoon.

To the proof.

"Stop kidding around, Sammy. You're going to be late for school." Mom turned to Dad. "We'd better get going too."

"Did *you* do it?" I asked Dad as he reached for his briefcase. "Did you eat my cereal? Did you move the spoon? Was it a joke?"

"You're reading too many ghost stories," Dad

said. "Way too many." Then he and Mom hurried off for work.

For a few minutes, I sat at the kitchen table. Just sat there, staring into my empty cereal bowl.

Someone ate my cereal.

I am *not* going crazy, I told myself.

Someone ate my cereal.

But who?

"Sammy. Sammy."

Huh?

"Sammy, would you like to tell us what is so fascinating outside?" Ms. Starkling crossed her arms in front of her, waiting for my answer.

A few kids giggled.

I had been gazing out the classroom window. Thinking — about *my* window. My *open* bedroom window. And my disappearing cereal.

"Uh — no. I mean nothing," I said. "I mean — I wasn't looking at anything."

Some more giggles.

"Sammy, come up to the chalkboard, please, and show the class how to finish this equation."

"But it's Roxanne's turn," I blurted out. "I mean, isn't Roxanne supposed to show the class today?"

"Sammy, please." Ms. Starkling tapped the chalkboard with a piece of chalk. "Now."

I glanced at Roxanne. She just shrugged her shoulders.

I was in big trouble.

I didn't do my math homework last night. And I didn't do it this morning either — because Brutus didn't wake me up on time.

My temples pounded as I made my way to the front of the classroom. I walked slowly. Staring at the equation. Trying to figure out how to solve it before I got up there.

I had no idea.

Ms. Starkling handed me the piece of chalk.

Silence fell over the classroom.

I stared hard at the numbers on the board.

My palms began to sweat.

"Read the equation out loud," Ms. Starkling suggested. She said it nicely. But I could tell she was losing her patience.

I read the equation out loud.

It didn't help.

I lifted the chalk to the board, even though I still didn't know what to do.

I stared at the numbers some more.

I heard the sound of kids shifting impatiently in their seats.

I placed the chalk against the board — and gasped.

I felt something squeeze my hand. Something cold and wet.

My knees started to shake.

I felt hot breath right up against my face.

I tried to step back — but I couldn't move.

Something squeezed my fingers tighter and tighter. Squeezed until it hurt.

The breathing against my face grew more rapid — sharp gasps that stung my cheeks.

I wanted to pull free. But then my hand started to move across the chalkboard.

My hand was moving — and it started to write!

Someone was writing numbers for me! Someone was holding my hand! Moving it! Solving the equation!

Someone I couldn't see!

6

I yanked my hand back. I jerked free of the clammy, invisible grip.

Then I dropped the chalk — and started screaming.

And ran from the room.

I ran into the hall. I leaned against the wall outside the classroom. My hands were shaking. My knees trembled.

I could still feel the cold, ghostly fingers wrapped around my hand.

I heard Roxanne inside — volunteering to finish the equation.

"Sammy." Ms. Starkling met me out in the hall. "What happened? Are you sick? Would you like to see the school nurse?"

"I'm — I'm not sick," I stammered.

I didn't want to explain what happened.

I couldn't explain it. I didn't even want to try.

"Are you sure you don't want to see the nurse?

You don't look well." Ms. Starkling felt my forehead.

"No. I'm okay," I lied. "I — I just felt a little dizzy — because I didn't eat breakfast this morning."

Ms. Starkling believed me. She sent me to the lunch room to get something to eat.

As I made my way down the hall, I could still feel the clammy hand gripping my fingers.

Still feel the hot breath on my face.

Still feel the cold force as it pushed my hand along the board. Guiding it. Writing the numbers for me.

I shivered.

Maybe Dad is right. Maybe I *have* been reading too many ghost stories.

I walked home alone after school. I wanted to be by myself. To think.

I heard footsteps behind me. Footsteps pounding the pavement. Running toward me.

"Sammy — wait up!" It was Roxanne.

I pretended I didn't hear her. I kept walking.

"Sammy!" Roxanne caught up — out of breath. "What happened to you today?"

"Nothing happened."

"Something happened," she insisted. "Something happened to you in math class."

"I don't want to talk about it," I told her.

"I'm really good at math," Roxanne said smugly. "I'd be happy to help you — if you don't understand it."

"I . . . don't . . . need . . . help," I replied through gritted teeth. I began to walk faster — but Roxanne kept up with me.

We didn't talk.

Finally, Roxanne broke the silence. "Let's go to the haunted house Saturday night. For our project. Okay?"

"Maybe. I have to get home now. I'll call you later to talk about it."

I broke into a run — and left Roxanne on the sidewalk, staring after me.

I wanted to get home.

I wanted to think about everything that had happened.

I wanted to think about it — by myself.

As I headed into the house, I wondered about my bedroom window. Would it be open? I made sure it was closed before I left this morning. But that didn't mean anything.

I started up the stairs. But I stopped when I heard Brutus meowing loudly in the kitchen. He always does that when he wants to go out.

"Okay. Okay. I'm coming."

Brutus started to wail.

"Hold it down, Brutus. I said I was —"

I stopped in the kitchen door.

There was Brutus — crouched on a chair. His fur stood straight up. He pulled back his lips in a menacing hiss.

I followed his gaze — and let out a shriek.

A pizza sat on the table.

A slice from the pie floated above the plate — floated up by itself.

I stared in shock as it rose higher and higher.

"Who — who's there?" I stammered. "I know someone is there! Who ARE you?"

Don't let any Goosebumps books CREEP past you!

❏ BAB56880-9	#43	The Beast from the East	$3.99
❏ BAB56881-7	#44	Say Cheese and Die–Again!	$3.99
❏ BAB56882-5	#45	Ghost Camp	$3.99
❏ BAB56883-3	#46	How to Kill a Monster	$3.99
❏ BAB56884-1	#47	Legend of the Lost Legend	$3.99
❏ BAB56885-X	#48	Attack of the Jack-O'-Lanterns	$3.99
❏ BAB56886-8	#49	Vampire Breath	$3.99
❏ BAB56887-6	#50	Calling All Creeps	$3.99
❏ BAB56888-4	#51	Beware, the Snowman	$3.99
❏ BAB56889-2	#52	How I Learned to Fly	$3.99
❏ BAB56890-6	#53	Chicken, Chicken	$3.99
❏ BAB56891-4	#54	Don't Go to Sleep	$3.99
❏ BAB56892-2	#55	The Blob That Ate Everyone	$3.99
❏ BAB56893-0	#56	The Curse of Camp Cold Lake	$3.99
❏ BAB62836-4		Tales to Give You Goosebumps Book & Light Set Special Edition #1	$11.95
❏ BAB26603-9		More Tales to Give You Goosebumps Book & Light Set Special Edition #2	$11.95
❏ BAB74150-4		Even More Tales to Give You Goosebumps Book and Boxer Shorts Pack Special Edition #3	$14.99
❏ BAB53770-9		The Goosebumps Monster Blood Pack	$11.95
❏ BAB50995-0		The Goosebumps Monster Edition #1	$12.95
❏ BAB93371-X		The Goosebumps Monster Edition #2	$12.95
❏ BAB60265-9		Goosebumps Official Collector's Caps Collecting Kit	$5.99
❏ BAB73906-9		Goosebumps Postcard Book	$7.95
❏ BAB73902-6		The 1997 Goosebumps 365 Scare-a-Day Calendar	$8.95
❏ BAB73907-7		The Goosebumps 1997 Wall Calendar	$10.99
❏ BAB88132-9		Still More Tales to Give You Goosebumps Scare Pack	$11.95
❏ BAB23795-0		More and More Tales to Give You Goosebumps (Book and Cap Pack)	$14.99

- -

Scare me, thrill me, mail me GOOSEBUMPS now!

Available wherever you buy books, or use this order form.
Scholastic Inc., P.O. Box 7502, 2931 East McCarty Street, Jefferson City, MO 65102

Please send me the books I have checked above. I am enclosing $_____ (please add $2.00 to cover shipping and handling). Send check or money order—no cash or C.O.D.s please.

Name _____ Age _____

Address _____

City _____ State/Zip _____

Please allow four to six weeks for delivery. Offer good in the U.S. only. Sorry, mail orders are not available to residents of Canada. Prices subject to change.

GB1196